THE DROSERA LEGACY

PROTECTED BY THE SHADOWS

BOOK ONE

N.A. ROSE

Edits by Morena Stamm

Cover Design by Zhandre Dex G. (MC Damon)

This book contains excessive use of swearing and violence and includes explicit love scenes.

FOR THE TWI-HARDS OUT THERE WHO NEVER OUTGREW VAMPIRES, BUT ENJOY THEIR BOOKS

WITH A LITTLE MORE SPICE THESE DAYS.

CHAPTER ONE

The edges of Ryon's lips curled upwards as he reached forward and affectionately tucked a strand of hair behind the woman's ear, eliciting a soft sigh from her. He wasn't smiling because of the kiss he was about to share with the human, however. No, he was smiling because he knew in a matter of minutes, the blood that coursed through her veins would be trickling down his throat.

He couldn't remember the woman's name, but that was irrelevant. They were both here for one thing, and that wasn't to exchange pleasantries. Ignoring the pull of scarred skin on his hand, Ryon gripped the back of her head and pressed his lips to hers. There was nothing romantic or sensual about the kiss—at least not from his end. It was just a process. A way to get from 'A' to 'B'. Her lips were warm against his own and when she let out a mewl, he knew he had her where he wanted her. She opened her mouth, and he promptly accepted the invitation, delving his tongue in to meet her own. Whilst the blonde stranger seemed to enjoy the kiss, Ryon thought it was...well, *meh*. He'd done this night after night, time and time again. And he had yet to find a human woman who stirred anything more inside him other than his need to feed.

She groaned into his mouth when he deepened the kiss, and when her fingers fumbled with the zip of his jeans, he promptly pushed her hands away. This wasn't about him. Well, in a way, it *was*—just not in the way she intended. Did he want sex? Of course, but not from a human. There were plenty of civilian female vampires around for that. And besides, he had a stronger urge that he needed to sate. *No*, this was about giving pleasure to take blood. A bit of *give and take*.

It was dark in the alley where they stood. The only light that reached them was the flickering lamp from the adjoining street, but that wasn't a problem for Ryon. He pulled back from the kiss and watched her eyes roll back when his fingers found the apex of her thighs. The thin material of her skirt was barely a barrier between them as he deftly worked her into a frenzy, just as he intended. It didn't take long for her to reach a point where coherence was no longer part of her vocabulary— and then he struck.

Tilting her head to the side, he opened his mouth and plunged his fangs into her soft flesh, moaning at the first taste of blood. The liquid was warm and sweet with a hint of alcohol. The woman's breath hitched, and she tensed, but he knew his fingers would distract her. And after a moment, they did. He felt the tension leave her body as she came apart in his arms, jolting with the explosion of pleasure. He smiled against her neck as he moved his hand to her shoulder, holding her still while she basked in the afterglow of what she'd felt...and he drank.

"Problem with the Reds. We need you downtown," a familiar male voice said from somewhere behind him. A vampire could fade from any location *to* any location, were it across town or across the kingdom. As long as they didn't fade into the sun, there was no limit to the distance they could fade to. And if there was a strong enough bond between two vampires, they could even fade directly to one another. Which most of the time was a convenient ability to have, at other times—like right now—it was annoying as hell.

Ryon let out a groan of frustration. It was his night off —or at least it was meant to be. Reluctantly, he released the woman's neck and ran his tongue over the puncture wounds, closing them. When Ryon stepped back, the woman looked up at him with wide eyes. She cautiously lifted her hand to her already healed neck, her expression a mix of confusion, fear, and...realisation. Rumours of vampire existence ran rampant through the humans in town, but so far, it was just that—a rumour. And that's how it had to stay.

Like all vampires, Ryon had the power to compel humans. He could twist their minds and make them believe things that never happened and forget things that had.

Holding her gaze, Ryon poured power into his words. "You're going to take your things and hail a cab from outside the club." The woman's eyes glazed over, and she nodded jerkily as Ryon continued to speak. "You're going to go home and get some sleep, and when you wake up, you won't remember me or what happened in this alley."

The woman nodded and picked up her bag and jacket from the ground beside her. Ryon watched, his eyes riveted to the woman's backside as she walked away in her figure-hugging black skirt. She had a backside that would make most human men's palms itch to touch it. *Too bad humans do nothing for me*, he thought. But he could still appreciate a good thing when he saw one.

"Don't you know it's rude to interrupt someone while they're eating?" Ryon asked. He turned around, wiping the remnants of blood from his lips with the back of his hand, as Kove stepped out from the shadows.

Kove was a beast of a male. Ryon maintained a muscular physique that would put any human man to shame, but Kove was something else entirely. He was slightly taller than Ryon and while Ryon maintained a clean-shaven jaw and short brown hair that was longer on top, Kove had a thick beard, and a mop of wild dark brown hair to match. He'd forgone his usual bun tonight, and the dishevelled waves now fell loosely to just above his shoulders. And like Ryon, Kove was a member of The Shadows.

The Shadows were a group of trained vampires whose duty was to enforce the rules set by the Vampire King—Cazimir Drosera. King Cazimir reigned over all Garabitha and although Kove, Ryon, and the seven other Shadow members lived in the small town of Ladwick, there were 'Shadows' stationed in various cities and towns all around Garabitha. No matter which city or town, the rules were the same, and they were set to keep vampires safe and their existence a secret from humans.

The rules were simple: One—Never kill a human. Two—Always wipe the memory of a human after feeding or...other interaction.

"Seemed like more than just eating," Kove replied, his casual tone doing nothing to hide the subtle judgement in his words.

The signature leather jacket Kove wore reflected off the

dim lighting of the alley as he stepped forward. All Shadows wore the same leather jacket with ribbed sleeves and a sheath across the back that held their other signature item—their sword. But while the other Shadows opted to wear jeans or slacks, Kove paired the leather jacket with...more leather.

"Nothing wrong with a bit of give and take," Ryon said with a smirk, his frustration ebbing as it made way for the easy banter that he was used to with Kove.

Kove's big body angled towards him, the leather creaking as his arms crossed over his chest. His dark eyebrows dropped, and those brown eyes flickered golden as they snapped to Ryon. "You're a Vampire. You don't need to give at all. Humans are there to be used. It's just a shame it's against the rules to kill them."

Ryon didn't care too much for humans, but he didn't hate them either. Not like Kove did. Kove's hate for them had turned to repulsion over the years and no one knew why. Kove was a friend—a close friend. Hell, they even lived together. All the Shadows did—but he also liked to keep his cards close to chest. And no matter how much everyone asked him about his past, he refused to speak about it.

Having been through this same conversation a thousand times over, Ryon ignored Kove's comment and crossed his own arms over his chest mockingly. "Seems to me that you envy how easily I can give pleasure to humans. Are you jealous of my skills, old friend?"

Beneath that thick beard, Ryon was sure Kove's lips pulled into a thin line. Kove glared at Ryon for a long moment before he said, "Fynn is waiting. Are you coming with us or not?"

Ryon sighed and let his arms fall by his side. "It's my night off. Why do you need me?"

"Some Reds downtown are causing trouble, and there could be too many of them for us to bring down without help."

'Reds' were vampires—aptly nicknamed for their signature scarlet red eyes—who had no control of their blood lust. It happened most often with newly made vampires, but at times, adult vampires lost control too and ultimately succumbed to their animalistic urges—Permanently. By the time a vampire's eyes turned red, they no longer possessed the ability to pull back from a feeding and they would drink until they drained their victims dry. And that's where the Shadows would come in.

As enforcers for the King, it was fitting for the Shadows to be the ones to put down the 'Reds' since only Kings possessed the Royal blood needed to turn humans into vampires. If a human died with even the smallest amount of royal blood within them, they would transition into a vampire and rise again.

"And the others?" Ryon asked, referring to the rest of the Shadow members.

Kove shook his head. "They're scattered around town, and you're the closest thing I've got. Fynn's already down there. Are you coming or not?"

Ryon didn't need to answer. They both knew he'd never leave a friend hanging. Ryon patted his jeans pocket and felt for the switch blade he carried as a backup. Being his night off, he'd left his sword back at the mansion, so he'd have to make do with what he had. He gave Kove a curt nod. "Right behind you."

CHAPTER TWO

Laina looked around the crowded nightclub. The lights were dimmed, but the strobes that flickered around the large room made it easy enough to see everyone. The music was loud and playing some pop song that had all the bodies on the dance floor bumping and grinding, and those who weren't dancing littered every other crevice of the club.

From her seat in the booth at the back of the room, Laina could see all the patrons' smiling faces. They were happy. Unlike Laina, they exuded vibrance and life as they talked, laughed, and danced with their friends on a regular Saturday night at the local club. They had no idea what Laina had gone through six months ago—or what she was still going through. And why should they? They were strangers, living their lives... and that was the problem. These strangers were living their lives while the two people who meant the most in the world to Laina were dead.

"Are you okay?" Max called out from across the booth. Laina glanced over at her best friend, and the reason she was out tonight at all. He was always observant and seemed to know precisely when Laina was stuck in her own thoughts. Max was incredibly handsome with brown hair and grey eyes that looked almost blue. And, as if he needed another thing going for him, he was sweet and an incredibly good listener. And for anyone else, Max was the perfect package. But for Laina, he was just her best friend.

Laina gave a half-hearted smile and lifted the empty glass in her hand. "I need a refill." She didn't *need* a refill. She needed space. She needed time. She needed her parents back.

"Do you need me to come with you?" he asked, his face a mask of concern.

She shook her head. "No, I'll be fine."

She felt Max's eyes on her as she shuffled out from the booth and shouldered her handbag. Max's friends remained in the booth, continuing their conversation as she headed for the bar. She wouldn't ruin tonight for Max. Tonight was about celebrating his new job at Lunar Productions—Ladwick's most sought-after Digital Animation Companies. Max and Laina met in college, and both went on to study design. When they graduated, they found good-paying jobs in the industry, but while Max was moving up in the world, Laina was the opposite. After what happened six months ago, she lost her initiative to work, to see her friends, to do...well, anything really. She fell into a dark hole of depression and numbness that still consumed her to this day. Laina had lost contact with all her friends besides Max, and she lost her job. She moved into freelancing just to pay the rent, but the truth was, she found no enjoyment in it anymore. In fact, she found no joy in doing anything anymore.

Laina pushed past the hordes of people to get to the bar. She ordered herself a refill of wine and, as soon as the bartender brought it over, she downed the liquid in one hit. She wasn't a big drinker, but she could do with the buzz tonight.

"Are you sure you're okay?" Max asked from behind her.

Laina turned to face him. "Stop worrying about me. I'm fine."

"I don't want you to feel uncomfortable," he said, placing a tentative hand on her shoulder. "I can take you home if you'd like?"

Laina's phone buzzed in the back pocket of her jeans, but she ignored it. Shaking her head, she said, "no, Max. Honestly, I'm fine. I'm just going to freshen up a bit in the ladies', and I'll meet you back at the table, okay?"

Max's lips thinned, as if he was trying to decide what to do. He glanced at their table before returning his gaze to her. "Are you sure?"

"Yes, absolutely." She plastered a smile on her face and placed a hand over his. "My best friend just accepted an offer on his dream job. We should be celebrating! I'll get the next round."

He chuckled as she pulled her hand away and he released her shoulder. "There's already enough alcohol at the table." After a moment he added, "well, when you're ready to go home, just say the word, and we're out of here. Deal?"

She nodded. "Deal."

She watched Max's slim form walk back to the table. He wasn't exactly a gym junkie, but she knew he enjoyed working out most days—and it showed. His collared shirt pulled taut against his shoulders and biceps, showing off the powerful muscles that he hid underneath. He truly was the perfect package, and sometimes Laina wished she saw him that way, but she didn't. He was like a brother to her, and besides, she didn't feel that way about anyone. Because to feel that way would mean she would have to feel something at all. And Laina felt nothing—well, not *exactly* nothing. She felt fear, sadness, and anxiety well enough. But the truth was, she hadn't felt anything akin to happiness ever since that night, six months ago.

Laina made her way to the ladies' room. She could still hear the thumping bass of the music as she leaned back against the closed door, but at least the pounding beats were somewhat muffled from here. She was alone. *Finally.*

She closed her eyes and was immediately taken back to that night when everything changed. She didn't mean to think about it, but the loud music, the smell of sweat and cigarettes, and the thrum of vibrations sent her spiralling into a memory she'd rather forget. She had been standing in the ladies' room just like this one. She could still remember how the voice of the unknown caller was so soft that she had to lock herself in the farthest cubicle from the door just to hear. At the time, she had been slightly drunk and missed the beginning of the conversation, but she had sobered instantly when she heard the words. F

"...the daughter of Elizabeth and Liam Hawkins? We need you to come to Oak Hills to identify the body of a man and woman that we believe may be your parents."

Laina opened her eyes when she felt a continuous string of vibrations from her back pocket, the phone call sending her catapulting back to reality. She let out a sigh and reached into her pocket. Unlike that call six months ago, she knew exactly who was calling this time.

"Brynn," Laina said grudgingly, answering the call.

"I've been trying to call you!" Brynn, her sister, blasted into the phone. Laina winced and pulled the phone away from her ear. Being both a police officer and her older sister, Brynn had an authority complex that meant she continuously needed to check in with Laina on the daily. Her sister continued, "where are you? I've been trying to get in touch with you. What's that sound? Is that...music? Are you out?"

"Yes, I'm out. I'm with Max and a few of his friends," Laina said. She made her way over to the basin and took in her reflection in the mirror on the wall. The dark circles under her eyes were evidence of her lack of sleep and her hollow cheeks were still obvious despite the blush she'd remembered to put on. The once vibrant green colour of her eyes seemed almost dull now. As she waited for Brynn's response, she reached up and touched the frown line between her brows. *That's new.*

"Do you know how dangerous it is to be out at night?" Brynn replied. "You have no *idea* how bad it is out there! I do!"

The door to the ladies' room swung open, and in walked —no, in *stumbled*—two platinum blonde girls that looked barely old enough to drink. They giggled, leaning on each other as they found their way to their own stalls.

"Hello?" Brynn prompted.

Laina walked over to the far wall and lowered her voice. "I am not your responsibility. I'm not a child, Brynn, and you need to stop treating me like it."

"Look, Laina, I'm trying to look out for you." The silence between them stretched out before Brynn added, "just be careful, and let me know when you get home. Okay?"

"Will do," Laina replied.

Brynn was never one to show emotion growing up. Laina

was always the one who wore her heart on her sleeve, but now that she'd wrapped that heart of hers in a blanket of concrete and closed herself off from the world emotionally, it was obvious Brynn had no idea how to tackle it. Maybe that's why she'd become so controlling.

Ever since their parents died, Brynn had tried to step into their shoes. She'd tried to be a parent to Laina in a way one would a young child. She would call her constantly, berate her about her choices, and tell her what to do.

But Laina wasn't a child. She was thirty years old and had lived independently for six years, yet Brynn couldn't see that. Of course, Laina was under no impression that Brynn had it easy since their parents' death. The last six months had been tough for the both of them, and the lack of closure surrounding their deaths hadn't helped any. They were murdered. There was no motive, no weapon, no fingerprints, or DNA other than her parents' own, and no perpetrator—besides, what the locals claimed.

"Okay," her sister said after a moment. "I guess I'll speak to you later."

"Okay, bye," Laina said, breaking the awkward silence by ending the call.

She put the phone in her back pocket and repositioned her handbag before glancing at her reflection in the mirror. She didn't even recognise the woman staring back at her, and it wasn't just because of the clear signs of tiredness across her face. There was a dark emptiness inside of her that was clear in the hollow and emotionless eyes that looked back at her.

The blonde girls from earlier took that moment to come out of their stalls, and Laina stood at the basin watching as they washed their hands and stumbled back outside. The rush of noise that briefly flooded the room made her cringe. She didn't feel like going back out there...but she would. For Max, she would. And she would plaster on a smile and pretend to feel something she didn't. After splashing water on her face and taking a few minutes to freshen up, Laina headed back to the booth.

"Ah, there you are," Max said from where he now stood, pulling on his coat. "How do you feel about getting some food? We're going to grab a bite to eat at that Italian place down the street. Would you be up for that?"

"Food sounds good," she said with a nod, remembering to smile. She took her coat from where it was draped over the booth and pulled it on as Max said goodbye to the rest of his friends. Apparently, only a few of them were going to dinner.

As they made their way outside the club and into the cool night air, Laina shivered, her denim jacket doing nothing to halt the winter chill from seeping in. Jeremy and...*Emma, was it?* were deep in conversation as they took the lead and started down the street, with Max and Laina following closely behind.

You have no idea how bad it is out there. Her sisters' words stuck with her as she took that moment to look around the empty streets. It was dark out. Very dark. The streetlamps were few and far between and cast shadows in every corner. It was eery and instantly reminded her of that night in Oak Hills. The last few months had seen an increase in murders overnight around Ladwick. As a police officer, Brynn had been at the scenes and told Laina how some bodies had the same puncture wounds at their necks and wrists as were found on their parents' bodies that night. There were whispers around town that the murders were the work of vampires, and when Brynn had first told Laina the theory, Laina had almost keeled over, laughing. *vampires.* Vampires were nothing more than a figment of someone's deranged imagination, and it had shocked Laina that Brynn had even entertained the idea.

"Laina?" Max's voice brought her attention back to the present, and she realised she had stopped walking.

She let out a breath and shook her head, pushing the thoughts aside. "Sorry, what—"

A woman's ear-piercing scream rang out, and both Laina and Max swung around to where Jerem—

"Where are your friends?" she asked in a whisper. Jeremy and Emma were nowhere to be seen. There was an alleyway ahead of them, but there was no reason for Jeremy or Emma to go down there—the restaurant was on the main street.

"They were right in front of us..." Max shook his head. A male's cry echoed in the night, and Max's head snapped to Laina, his eyes wide and filled with terror. "That-that sounded like Jeremy."

A wave of apprehension washed over Laina as more screams rang out. And before she knew what she was doing, her legs were moving. Her breaths grew shallow with every stride as she ran alongside Max towards the alley. Towards the screams.

CHAPTER THREE

Ryon appeared beside Kove in the back alley of the old Grand Hotel. He knew downtown Ladwick well enough to know that half of these buildings were abandoned. The other half were in the process of being luxuriously renovated in attempts to lift the area from an after-thought to a booming tourist destination. It would never be the latter, though. If the run-down buildings weren't being turned into nightclubs, they were overrun by vampires, just like this hotel. He could scent plenty of vampires and humans inside. Since the only fresh human blood he could smell nearby was coming from the entrance of this alley and not the hotel, which meant the vampires inside weren't a concern.

The sound of scuffling and hissing drew his attention to the six large figures in the alley hunched over four smaller limp forms. Even though it was dark, Ryon's vampire sight could easily see the glowing red eyes of the six vampires and the bodies of the humans on the ground. The Reds weren't just feeding. They were *feasting.*

"The humans were dead when I got here," a male voice

said from the side of the alley. "So, I figured I may as well wait for backup before pulling the plug on their party."

Ryon had already scented his friend, but he glanced over to see Fynn inhale from his half-smoked cigarette as he casually leaned back against the alley wall.

Fynn wasn't as broad-shouldered as the rest of the Shadows, and where Kove and Ryon had dark hair and dark features, Fynn had light brown hair that almost looked blond and a goatee to match. And unlike Ryon and Kove, Fynn liked to smoke. A lot. He was also one of the newer members of the Shadows, having joined the ranks around ten years ago.

"You know that will kill you?" Ryon said, pointing at the lit tab.

Fynn's blue eyes danced with humour, and he smiled. "Wouldn't want *that* to happen, would we?" He made a show of putting out his smoke before he gestured to the Reds. "Ready?"

Ryon raked his gaze over the four human men on the ground. Their skin was grey, their eyes wide open—and lifeless. As Fynn pointed out, these Reds had drained the humans —something that was against the rules set by the King. And something that was punishable by death.

An ear-piercing scream rang out, and Ryon tensed, immediately sensing the racing hearts of nearby humans. He glanced over at the feasting Reds to see a man and woman just inside the entrance to the alley. The woman had her hands to her mouth, the man beside her fumbling for something in his pocket. Witnesses. *Shit.*

Besides their scarlet-coloured eyes and their insatiable lust for blood, Reds were incredibly fast thanks to those animalistic urges they so heavily relied on. Within seconds, the four vampire's heads snapped up to the humans at the entrance to the alley. With a hiss, two of them faded, reappearing in the same place as they were, but now with the two new humans in their clutches. Screams rung out, echoing around the alley, and in the blink of an eye, all four Reds had their heads down as they began to feed.

Ryon was already moving when he yelled out, "Kill them!"

Pulling out the switchblade in one swift move, Ryon flipped it open and faded to just behind one of the vampires, slicing the blade along his throat. He could do a lot more damage with his trusty sword, but the switchblade would have to do. The woman fell to the floor as the vampire stumbled back, holding his throat. Despite dying of old age—*very* old age for a vampire—there were only two ways to kill one, through the heart or through the head. And with the short blade in Ryon's possession, he wasn't confident he'd be able to do either. But he'd try.

With one hand holding the handle and the other covering the hilt, he thrust the blade forward and into the Red's chest. *Bingo.* Ryon pulled out the blade as the vampire fell to the floor, but before Ryon could turn around, another Red launched itself onto his back, sending him stumbling forward.

The vampire's nails dug into his shoulder through the leather, and he felt the warm breath against his neck as the vampire prepared to bite. But Ryon wouldn't let him. Reds might have the advantage of speed, but Ryon had strength. He thrust his elbow against the vampire's head, sending the Red flying backwards. And then Kove was there.

Kove lifted his sword above his head and plunged it deep into the Red's chest cavity. Ryon glanced over at Fynn, and by the look of it, he'd already taken care of the other two Reds.

Ryon's ears pricked up at the faint sound of additional heartbeats. More humans? He swung around to the alley entrance just as another man and woman rounded the corner. He didn't pay much attention to the man, but the woman... there was something about the woman that...

An intoxicating scent didn't so much reach him as knock him over. Time stood still as his legs threatened to give out, but he somehow managed to stay standing.

Without taking his eyes off the woman, he closed the switchblade and put it in his pocket. She was...breath-taking. And her scent was no different. It was sweet, like a mix of vanilla and cinnamon with a hint of rose. He'd never scented anything like it. Her long brown hair hung loose in waves past her shoulders, and even in the dark shadows of the alley, he could clearly see her green eyes wide with shock as they took in the scene. Her cheeks were rosy from the chill of the night, and her full lips were the colour of the richest blood...And *damn*, that made him want her even more.

She wore a white t-shirt under a denim jacket with slim-fitting black jeans that hugged the most delicious curves he'd ever seen. The exposed skin of her collarbone caught his attention, and he found his gaze trailing up to her neck. He could *see* her racing heartbeat pulsing through that vein at her throat. Without willing it, his fangs shot out, throbbing with the need to pierce her skin as a jolt of desire ran through him. *What the hell?* He'd never had such a strong reaction to a female before —and certainly not a human. He was vaguely aware of Kove calling for a clean-up crew from somewhere behind him. Ryon should be helping them to wipe the humans' memories and do the clean-up. But he was frozen in place, his eyes locked on the woman.

"Ryon! The girl!" At Kove's voice, Ryon glanced back. Fynn was talking to the two *alive* humans, healing their bites, and wiping their minds, whilst Kove was sprinting towards the man standing at the alley entrance. It was then that Ryon glanced back at the woman and realised that somehow, he'd neglected to notice the phone she held in her hand.

He faded and appeared before her in a split-second and immediately regretted it. Her scent was stronger up close, and it threatened to overwhelm him. Her green eyes were a dark, mossy colour that made him think of the mountainside greenery in the hills outside Ladwick. When his gaze darted to her lips, he was captivated by the way her bottom one was slightly fuller than the top. Her facial features were petite and feminine, and for a human, her skin was pale but naturally flawless. Naturally *beautiful*.

Her eyes widened on him as she backed up to the alley wall.

"You don't want to do that," he drawled, stalking up to her. He reached out and took the phone from her before she could stop him.

She frowned and tracked the phone, but when she looked back up at him, he didn't see the fear in her eyes that he expected from a human in this situation. Instead, she looked annoyed.

"Is it money that you want?" she asked as she lifted the small handbag from her shoulder and shuffled through it.

"What?" Ryon almost laughed. "No, I don't want your money."

He watched as she swallowed hard, shouldering her handbag once more. "Are...are you going to kill us?"

Us? Ryon glanced over his shoulder at the man Kove was

speaking to and most likely wiping his memory. Was this woman with him? A sudden pang of anger ran through him at the thought. Was he...jealous? *No,* he couldn't be jealous. She was a stranger—a human, for fuck's sake. Yes, a *pretty* human, but a human, nonetheless. And he had no interest in her. None whatsoever. He needed to wipe her mind and be done with it...but instead he found himself asking, "what's your name?"

"Are you going to kill us?" she asked again, ignoring his question. Her voice was stronger now and he couldn't help but think she was brave to face him like this, asking her question so directly. Most humans cowered when faced with a vampire...at least until they had their minds wiped, that was. *Which is what I should be doing right now.*

He gave a slight shake of his head. "No, I have no plans to kill you."

Her eyebrows lowered briefly, and she leaned to the side to look around him. He followed her movement, using his body to block her view. For some strange reason, he felt a sudden urge to protect her from the brutality of what had gone down behind him.

"But you killed those people," she said unabashed, her eyes flicking back up to his.

It wasn't a question, but he replied anyway. Something twisted deep inside his gut at the thought of this woman believing he was a murderer. Well, actually...he was. He just didn't murder innocents.

"We didn't kill the..." he caught himself before he said 'humans'. He was vaguely aware of Kove calling out his name, but he ignored it. "What's your name?" he asked again, not knowing why it felt so important for him to know.

20

She didn't give him an answer, instead she leaned further to the side. "But the bodies..."

He moved to block her view again but froze when she stretched out, craning her neck to the side, causing her long hair to fall forward and expose the skin at her neck. Unintentionally, Ryon's gaze lowered to the pale flesh of her neck and locked on the pulsating vein there.

The scent of her human blood called to him. It was alluring and all-consuming, making it impossible to hold back...The low snarl that escaped him was one of pure need. And not just from a feeding perspective. He wanted her in every way possible. His lips pulled back over his sharpened fangs, and he could barely stop himself from plunging them into her fragile neck.

At the sound of his snarl, she pulled back and looked up at him. Her eyes went round when she met gaze and then glanced at his lengthened fangs. He could pinpoint the moment she realised *what* he was.

She slammed back against the alley wall so hard it made him wince. "You're...you're..." the woman stuttered, barely more than a whisper. Her eyes were wide, and he saw pure fear in them. She darted a look over his shoulder. "*No.*" She met his gaze once more, her face blanching at the realisation. "No. Not possible."

Okay. Now was the time to wipe this woman's memory. Now was the time to erase himself from the depths of her mind and make her forget about everything she'd seen. He called forth his ability to compel and opened his mouth to begin...but stopped. He couldn't bring himself to do it. He didn't *want* to do it. There was something different about this human. Something that made a selfish part of him creep to the surface and be willing to break those ever-important rules made by the King just so she could remember him.

"You have to get out of here," he said low. What the hell was he doing?

"You're not going to hurt me?" she asked, her tone filled with disbelief.

"No...I'm not going to hurt you," he said, leaning in until they were a hairbreadth away from each other. Her eyes searched his, and he saw a heaviness in her green gaze, a burden of sorrow or grief. She'd been through something. She'd experienced something that had tainted her very being. And at that moment, he decided he *would* let her go.

"You have to leave," he said, ensuring there was no compulsion in his words. Kove and Fynn would look over at any moment, and being this close to her, it would look as though he were using compulsion. The woman's breath hitched, and Ryon suppressed a shudder at how close their bodies were. How close their lips were...

"Do not tell anyone what you have seen tonight. If you do, I won't hurt you, but others might. When you leave, your friends—your *boyfriend*," he tacked on, but she didn't react, telling him nothing. *And why the hell do I even care if she has a boyfriend?*

"They won't remember anything that has happened here, but you will. Can I trust you not to say anything?"

Her next breath came out ragged, and after a moment, she gave a curt nod.

He ran his gaze over every inch of her face, wanting to remember it, to memorise it. And then he stepped back. Being a vampire meant his body no longer needed to work like a human's. He didn't need the oxygen in his lungs or his heart to pump the blood for his body to work—but muscle memory was a wonderful thing, and a vampire's body still worked as it had as a human. It just didn't need to. And thank the human God for that because he felt his heart stop as the woman began to walk away.

But then she halted and glanced over at him, her green eyes locking on his once more. "Laina," she said. "My name is Laina."

Ryon's heart was abruptly brought back to life as sure as if it had been defibrillated. He watched, his heart now pounding wildly in his chest as Laina walk away from him.

Laina, he thought. A beautiful name for a beautiful woman. It was a shame he'd never see her again. His chest ached at the thought, and he frowned at the feeling. He'd never been affected by a human in this way. Never felt emotions like these before.

"Calling Soran now for a clean-up crew," Fynn said, dragging Ryon's attention away from the woman as she left the alley with her friends.

"We should probably head back to the manor and give Soran a brief of what happened here," Kove said, glancing over at Ryon.

Ryon pushed down the feeling of guilt that seeped into his stomach under Kove's scrutinising gaze. Had Kove heard? Did he know that Ryon just broke one of the King's two rules? For a moment, he considered whether he'd made the right decision, letting Laina go with her memory intact.

Still, when he recalled how she'd looked at him with those mesmerising green eyes, he realised there was no decision to be made. He couldn't bring himself to mess with her mind like that. He just couldn't. And he had no idea *why*.

Ryon nodded at Kove. "Let's go."

He waited for Kove and Fynn to fade out before glancing back at the entrance to the alley, where Laina had turned the corner. Her scent still lingered, and he closed his eyes, inhaling as if he could preserve it inside his mind and body. A sudden vibration in his palm had him opening his eyes and glancing down, suddenly remembering the phone in his hand. Laina's phone.

CHAPTER FOUR

Laina fought the urge to glance back at the vampire as she rounded the corner of the alley. *Vampire. Vampires are real.* She looked up to where Max, Jeremy, and Emma had walked on ahead, oblivious to what had occurred. Laina wanted to scream out to them but the way they were talking and going about life as normal, made her realise the vampire was right. They didn't remember anything. They were *made* to forget.

She swallowed the knot in her throat as her mind reeled with the revelation. She couldn't believe it. She had laughed in Brynn's face when her sister had mentioned the theories, and yet here she was...owing her life—and her memory—to one of their kind.

When she'd been approached in that alley, she'd honestly thought she was about to die. And a part of her had been... okay with that at first. She'd be lying if she said the thought of seeing her parents again hadn't crossed her mind. But then the man, *no*, the vampire, had let her go. And she couldn't work out why.

Laina stopped walking as her mind returned to her parents. Their lifeless bodies, the theories of what had killed them, the recent murders, and everything that had happened only minutes ago. If vampires were real—and now she knew they were—then what had happened to her parents...

As reality sunk in, she felt as though the ground had crumbled beneath her feet. She reached out and leaned heavily against the wall of a store and realised they were almost at the restaurant.

"And we're here!" Laina heard Max say from a short distance away. He was standing at the Italian restaurant they had set out for, which now felt like a lifetime ago. Jeremy and Emma walked inside as Max stopped in the doorway, holding the door open. "Are you still up for dinner?" he asked, hopeful, as a chorus of conversations drifted outside. She glanced through the window to see table after table occupied with groups of people, all laughing and smiling and having a good time as they ate. They had no idea that vampires had just fed from and killed people half a block away.

"Laina?" Max called out, snapping her out of the train of thought.

Your friends won't remember anything that has happened here, but you will. The vampire's words circled her mind, and she wondered why her friends had their memories wiped yet hers remained untouched.

She plastered on a smile. "Of course!" she replied. "You go ahead. I'm just going to check in with Brynn."

"Are you sure?" he asked, sounding slightly concerned.

"Yeah. I'll be right in." She heard the door to the restaurant close, and she lifted her handbag, rummaging through it...

"Dammit!" she said through gritted teeth when she recalled that vampire had—

"Looking for this?" a deep, familiar voice said from behind her. Every inch of her body tensed as she slowly turned around to face the vampire from the alley. Did he change his mind about wiping her memory? About killing her?

The illumination from the nearby streetlamp made it easier to see the vampire, and she couldn't help but take him in —all of him. He was tall with broad shoulders and looked powerfully strong in his black leather jacket that did nothing to hide the thick biceps underneath. He had dark brown hair that was longer on top, and she had a fleeting thought that it was long enough to run her hands through it.

She inwardly cursed at herself for even thinking something like that. She couldn't deny that he was handsome. *Incredibly* handsome. He had dreamy light brown eyes that looked made for the bedroom and seemed to glow a golden colour. Was that a vampire trait? He had thick eyebrows that hooded those eyes, a powerful jaw, and a straight nose. His masculine features and slightly tanned skin made him look more like a warrior than a vampire. His leather jacket had ribbed sleeves to the cuff and the black shirt he wore under it was pulled taut across his chest, showing off the ridges of his pecs.

And when she drew her gaze lower, she noticed his muscular body tapered into a slim waist where his dark blue jeans hung low.

"Like what you see?" he asked smugly. Laina's head snapped up to see the corners of his lips curl up into a smirk as he crossed his arms over his chest, showing her just how muscular he truly was.

She narrowed her eyes on him as his words sunk in. *So, he's cocky too.* Maybe when it came to men, vampires and humans weren't so different after all. She stayed where she was as he strode right up to her. Lifting her chin, she tried to calm her racing heart. She wasn't scared. *No*, her heart rate had nothing to do with fear and everything to do with the sudden surge of excitement that ran through her. *Why am I...excited?*

"It's okay, you know. To like what you see? Because..." his voice drifted off as his gaze lowered, his eyes taking in every inch of her body and leaving a trail of fire in its wake. "I sure as hell like what I see."

Laina feigned a scoff and glanced down, noticing her phone in his hand. She snatched it out of his grip, her eyes lingering on the skin there. Raised ridges on his flesh caught the light, and she couldn't tell if it was just a shadow or...scars?

"Laina?"

Laina tore her eyes from the vampire's and swung around to see a concerned Max. She'd completely forgotten about Max, the restaurant, and everything, really.

"Laina, are you okay?" Max asked as he came up to her.

"She's fine," the vampire answered curtly before she could reply.

"Who's this?" Max demanded. At Max's words, Laina couldn't help but glance back at the vampire. Her gaze locked on his as she felt something like a...a *connection* forming between them. Like a bond, or a secret that only the two of them knew about—well, that last one wasn't too far from the truth, was it?

"Ryon. My name is Ryon," the vampire replied without taking his eyes off her. She had the vaguest impression that he'd said that to *her*, not Max. And for some ridiculous reason, she noticed the slight fluttering of butterflies inside her stomach.

"Well, *Ryon*," Max spat the last word. "*We* are late for dinner." Max placed an arm over her shoulder and Laina saw the vampire—*Ryon's*—eyes follow the movement as his jaw clenched. Was he...jealous? And why did that thought only make the butterflies flutter even more? Max leaned down to whisper, "Laina, we should go."

Laina snapped out of whatever trance she was in and nodded at Max. "Yeah." She pulled out from under Max's arm, noticing that the vampire's expression seemed to relax as she did so. "Thanks for...*finding* my phone."

Ryon ducked his head and the edges of his lips curled up on a tight-lipped smile before he said, "you're welcome, Laina."

She felt a flicker of excitement as she allowed Max to guide her away from Ryon. Her eyes glazed over as she walked away, her mind reeling from everything over the last hour. She replayed all that had happened, minute by minute and second by second as she followed Max inside the restaurant and over to their table.

She was vaguely aware of Max talking, but she couldn't focus on what he was saying. Instead, she recalled the gentle-man-like dip of Ryon's head and how her name had rolled off his tongue like a sensual caress. She had reacted to him—mind and body. He was handsome, intriguing and there was something about him that almost fooled her into forgetting that he was a vampire. *Almost.*

CHAPTER FIVE

Ryon appeared on the front lawn of the manor to see Fynn and Kove impatiently waiting for him at the base of the stairs that led to the entrance. Kove leaned back against the railing, his arms crossed over his chest and a look of pure annoyance on his face while Fynn paced the bottom step with a cigarette in his mouth.

"Took you long enough," Kove remarked as Ryon approached.

Ryon shrugged as he continued up the steps past Kove. "Had something I needed to do." If he acted casual, maybe they wouldn't suspect anything was amiss—like the fact that he'd let the human woman walk away without wiping her memory.

"Like that human girl?" Kove asked. Ryon stopped mid-step as his gut twisted with worry. Not for himself, but for what would happen to Laina if Kove or the others found out, and it got back to the King. The King would track her down, and he wouldn't just wipe her memory—he'd likely turn her into an example. And then Ryon would be the one to be put down.

Ryon inwardly cursed at the thought. How had he been so stupid? Why didn't he just wipe her memory and be done with it? His stomach coiled in knots as he began to regret his decision...Hell, what was the difference anyway? It's not like he'd see her ever again—even though he'd like to.

"One of these days, you're going to fuck up," Kove said, and it took Ryon a moment to realise the gravity in his words. Kove *didn't* know about Laina. And when Ryon glanced at Fynn, the uninterested expression on his face told Ryon that he didn't know either. *Thank the human God.*

Ryon slowly swung around, struggling to maintain the casual façade that he so desperately needed right now. "And why is it you care so much if I fuck up?"

"You know the rules," Kove gritted out. "I don't want you to be the reason humans find out about our existence."

Ryon stepped down until he was nose to nose with Kove. "Don't you think I know the rules?" Ryon asked, his tone sounding like more of a growl than words. "I fucking enforce them."

Kove didn't back down. He didn't even flinch. Squaring up to Ryon, he retorted, "Then why are you so nice to them? One day you'll be *too* nice and fuck up! You're a vampire, yet you lower yourself for these humans, these...*parasites.*"

Ryon tried to rein in his fury, but Kove was always harping on about Ryon being too nice to humans and he'd had enough. "You're afraid, aren't you?" he asked in a low, calm voice as Kove went to turn away.

"What?" Kove snapped, looking back.

"You hate humans so much that you've become afraid of

them," he said. Kove's eyes narrowed, but Ryon persisted, "haven't you?"

"*Afraid*?" Kove sneered. "I have every reason to hate them and it's not because I'm *fucking* afraid!"

"What's the reason then? Huh?" Ryon demanded, taking a step down to face Kove once again. Kove's fangs lengthened as he squared up to Ryon, but Ryon wasn't backing down.

"Alright. That's enough, boys." Fynn took that moment to stomp out his cigarette and come up beside them. "Unless you want everyone to know your business, I suggest you both shut up now," Fynn said.

Ryon heard the distant sound of voices and tore his gaze from Kove's to look over at the front lawn of the manor where Xavier, Malik, and Rune had faded in. It took Kove a few more seconds to disengage before they all turned to face the others, acting as if nothing had happened.

"You guys finished for the night?" Fynn called out as they approached.

"Yeah," Malik replied, his blue eyes stark in the night. "We're just here to get cleaned up, then we're heading out for food." And by food, they weren't talking about a fast-food run. The mansion had its own stash of human blood bags, but it didn't compare to the real thing. It was then that Ryon caught the scent of vampire blood, and lots of it. *Reds.* As the three Shadow members got closer, he could see their clothes and faces stained with the crimson liquid that came from a messy night of patrolling.

"More trouble with the Reds?" Ryon asked.

Malik nodded. "Five of them going nuts at a bachelor party in Millsgate."

Ryon's brows dropped on a frown. "It's happening more often."

It was Xavier that replied as they approached the stairs. "I know. And I don't know why. Most of them were recently transitioned too, going by their scent. It's like something's changed with the process."

Xavier shook his head, drawing Ryon's attention back to him. "All it'll take is one Red that gets past us and then we're all fucked. It would be all over the human news by dawn, and then we're sitting ducks while the sun's up."

Ryon was inclined to look over at Kove to assess his reaction, but he held back. Kove's *prediction* that Ryon would 'fuck up' would be the least of their concerns if their problem with the Reds kept up.

Xavier and the others said their goodbyes as Ryon, Kove, and Fynn made their way up the stairs and into the manor. He could hear Fynn and Kove behind him, talking, as he made his way down the long hallway and up the stairs towards Soran's office. Windows lined the stone walls, and as Ryon took in the red velvet drapes that were permanently pulled closed, he suddenly wondered if there were windows behind them at all. It's funny, he'd never spared a thought about those drapes and the would-be—or would be not—windows underneath, but now he seemed to be looking at everything in a new light.

He had enforced the King's rules without question for almost fifty years, but now with the increasing issue with the Reds, it felt as though things were changing. Hell, even his friendships were changing. With Kove's hate growing stronger by the day and with more Reds out there, threatening their ability to stay hidden from humans, it felt as though the vampire society in Ladwick was on the precipice of something big. Something that he couldn't quite put his finger on.

And then there was *Laina*. The human woman who he'd known for all of two minutes and had caused him, after fifty long years, to break one of the very rules that he was duty-bound to enforce. Maybe he should track her down and rectify that. Maybe he should find her again and wipe her memory. Malik was the tech guru in the manor and could easily use his resources to track any human or vampire down. *Yes, that's it.*

Ryon pushed down the sudden ache in his chest at the thought of Laina not remembering him. He had no idea why she affected him so, but at least in tracking her down and wiping her memory, it would give him an excuse to see her one last time. *Yes. He'd do it.* He would ask Malik to find her address and then he would pay her a visit. And wipe her memory.

As Ryon continued down the hall, he turned his attention to the red patterned rug that spanned the length of the corridor and the intricate patterns that made up the Royal Crest of King Cazimir Drosera. Like the drapes, he'd never noticed how the C and D were subtly wrapped in golden thorns that intertwined and repeated themselves in the form of ornate patterns as it continued down the runner.

"You kind of look like him, you know," Fynn said from behind him. Ryon stopped walking and swung around, realising he'd been too up in his head to notice his friends had stopped following him. Kove was down the hall frowning at his phone as he typed away, and Fynn was standing off to the side, running his hand down his goatee as he stared up at a painting on the wall.

"What?" Ryon asked Fynn as he backtracked to where they had stopped.

"I have to go," Kove said abruptly, causing Fynn and Ryon to glance over. "The D's need help with Zane." Zane was the newest member of the Shadows, having been sent here by the King about six months ago and was probably the only Shadow member who hated humans more than Kove. Being a relatively new vampire, Zane still struggled to maintain his blood lust and once or twice before, the Shadows had to pull him back from a feeding that wouldn't end. And it looked like now was another one of those times.

"Guess we'll see you back here later," Fynn said. Ryon kept quiet. He had nothing to say to Kove, and by the way Kove gave him one last glance, he too, knew how strained their fifty-year friendship had become.

When Ryon and Fynn reached Soran's office, the door was open, and they approached to see the head of the Shadows sitting behind his desk with pursed lips and a deep frown marring his face. Behind him, the enormous wall of CCTV cameras ran a continuous live feed of the manor's grounds. It continued to flick from image to image, showing nothing out of the ordinary.

Ryon stopped and took in the male that had been something of a father figure for his entire vampiric life. Ryon met Soran almost a century ago after he was turned into a vampire. One of the myths humans had wrong about vampires? They aged and died naturally—if they weren't killed beforehand—it just took close to three or four centuries to get there. And as Ryon looked over at the now older looking Soran, he wondered how much time he had left with the male. After the transition, Soran took care of Ryon. He'd taught him the ways of vampire society, how to control his blood lust, and he'd trained him. And fifty years ago, when the King had made the rules and formed the group of enforcers that were now called the Shadows, Soran stepped forward, with Ryon in tow.

To this day, Ryon had never met the King personally. Still, Soran often travelled to the palace and, as a result, had become one of the King's highly regarded advisers. And maybe that had something to do with how stressed he seemed to be lately. Soran's perfectly groomed dark grey hair was mussed, and his black eyebrows were drawn in low over his brown eyes as he looked down at one of the many papers on his desk.

"Come in," Soran said without glancing over at them.

When Ryon and Fynn took up the chairs in front of the desk, Soran finally looked up. "Where's Kove?" he asked.

"Zane," Fynn said as if the word alone was answer enough. And it was. Soran nodded and leaned back in his chair.

"I know it was your night off," Soran said, his eyes softening as he locked eyes with Ryon. "Thank you for helping out. How did it go?"

Ryon gave a nod. "Same deal. Just like the last ones, they had red eyes and no control over what they were doing. We caught them in the middle of an all-you-can-eat-human-buffet."

"It's happening more and more," Fynn said as he leaned back and crossed one leg over the other. "And a lot of them seem to be just out of their transition. Has something changed with the transitioning process? We didn't have this problem a year ago."

Soran scratched the back of his neck but didn't answer Fynn's question, likely because he didn't have the answer. Although Soran had become an advisor to the King, he wasn't privy to the transition process of turning a human into a vampire. In fact, no one but the King was.

"So, what do we do?" Ryon asked, leaning forward to rest his elbows on his knees. "Do we just keep putting them down?"

"At this stage," Soran answered simply. Ryon watched as Soran leaned back in his chair with a sigh. "The King won't appreciate us questioning him, but I think it's time I visit the palace and ask him directly."

"Do you need me to come with you?" Ryon had no actual interest in meeting the King, but his instinct told him not to let Soran go alone. As Shadows, they were taught never to question the King's authority, but something wasn't right. Things truly were changing—even Soran felt it.

Soran shook his head. "No, I'll be fine. I'll leave soon and be back before sunrise. Anyway," Soran continued, "unless there's something else, I need to get back to all this admin work that I love so much." Those dark brown eyes looked from Ryon to Fynn. "No? Okay then. Close the door behind you."

Ryon and Fynn left Soran's office and made their way down the hall and up the stairs to where each of the Shadow members had their own room. When Fynn said his goodbye's and headed for his bedroom, Ryon was glad for it. He wasn't up for company right now. He had big plans to have a glass of whiskey and forget all about that pretty little human woman called Laina with the big green eyes and the long brown hair. At least until Malik returned to the manor.

CHAPTER SIX

Laina could feel Ryon's lips against hers. They were softer and warmer than she expected and when she parted her lips, he knew exactly what to do. Without hesitation, he delved in and began exploring her mouth with his tongue as his hand came up to cup the back of her head.

But then he abruptly pulled back.

She opened her eyes and was met with his light brown ones that now seemed to glow a golden colour.

"Laina," Ryon whispered in that deep voice. That voice...it sent ripples of excitement and anticipation through her.

"Laina!" he said louder. She frowned at the sudden volume increase. *Why was he yelling?*

"Laina!" *That doesn't sound like Ryon at all.*

"Laina! I swear to God, you better open this door now or I'm going to break it down and I *know* you don't have the money to fix it!"

Oh shit! Brynn!

Laina's eyes sprung open, and it took her a moment to

realise she was in her bed, in her apartment...*alone*. And Brynn was knocking on her door.

"Okay, Laina, that's it. I'm coming in! One...two..."

Laina sprung forward and ran out into the living room so fast that she tripped on her handbag and body-slammed the front door. "I'm coming!" She unlocked the deadbolt and pulled open the door as an unimpressed Brynn stormed inside.

"What the hell, Laina?" Brynn demanded as Laina closed the door. "You were meant to call me when you got home last night. I was freaking out that something had happened to you or that you were injured or worse! I've been calling and texting, and my last resort was to come here and break down your door!"

Laina scrubbed her hands over her face, trying to get her brain to wake up enough to focus. She walked back to the armchair and sat down. "I...uh...I must have put my phone on silent at some stage. What time is it?"

"It's seven a.m." Brynn said as she sat down on the adjoining lounge and looked up at Laina. Those big brown eyes, the same colour as their mother's, did nothing to hide the bags underneath. Her short brown hair was tucked behind her ears and by the way some of the strands stuck out, it looked like she'd had a hard night.

It was then that Laina noticed Brynn was still in her blue police uniform. "And before you ask, I left your spare key at home and since I couldn't get in touch with you, I came straight here after my night shift." Brynn leaned forward, the tiredness in those eyes immediately replaced with concern. "Are you okay? What happened last night?"

"Last night, I..." Laina's voice trailed off as she recalled the alleyway. The bodies. The vampire—*Ryon*. She should tell

Brynn. She should tell her everything. But then Laina recalled Ryon's words: *Do not tell anyone what you have seen tonight. If you do, I won't hurt you, but others might.*

"Last night you...?" Brynn prompted.

She shrugged. "Last night, I had a good time. And I didn't text you because I pretty much passed out when I got home." *Not a lie.* After they finished at the restaurant, Max had dropped her off at home and she'd showered, taken off her makeup, and, despite everything, had fallen asleep the moment her head hit the pillow.

Laina's thoughts drifted back to Ryon. She wouldn't tell Brynn about what happened, but she could try to get some more information. "When I spoke to you last night, you said things were getting really bad out on the streets." Brynn nodded gravely as if she didn't want the reminder. "What did you mean? Have there been more bodies?"

"Yeah, more bodies. And it seems to be growing in number each night." Brynn shook her head. "Each body has been found with the same twin puncture wounds but in various places—their necks, their arms, their wrists." She ran a hand through her short brown hair and sighed. "It only gives those paranormal fanatics more reason to believe their theories."

"Theories," Laina repeated absentmindedly, dropping her gaze to the floor. *Not just theories anymore.* Looking back up at her sister, she asked, "do you believe them?"

"It's not that I believe it. I mean, after what happened to..." *our parents*, Laina filled in, "...it's hard not to feed into those theories. Even the detectives are stumped. When the bodies are found, there's never evidence of a scuffle, no DNA other than the victims' own, no tracks from footprints or getaway cars, and most importantly no witnesses." She sighed again and leaned forward. "I just don't know what to believe anymore."

After a moment of silence Brynn stood up. "Anyway, now that I know you're alive and well, I'll head home for some sleep."

Laina stood up and walked her sister to the door. She normally had more energy to fight with Brynn about constantly checking in on her, but this time, she just said, "Thanks for checking in on me."

Brynn stopped and blinked at Laina, clearly confused by the sudden gratitude. They said their goodbyes and then Brynn was gone, leaving Laina alone.

Letting out a sigh, Laina walked over to the patio curtains and threw them open. Usually, she hated letting in the morning sun—it was a reminder of what her parents could no longer experience. But now, she felt different about it; now, sunlight meant...*safety*. Or at least she thought it did if the rumours about vampires and sunlight were true. She looked out at the street below, the people going about their daily routines and commutes to work with no idea that creatures that were known only in folklore tales now walked among them at night.

Making her way to the bathroom, she had a quick shower to wake herself up, pulled her hair into a bun on top of her head, and put on her favourite outfit—some jeans and an oversized black sweater.

When she was done, she sat down at the kitchen bench and opened her laptop. She had two freelance graphic design projects that needed to be completed and a few more that she'd scheduled in. And hopefully she would earn enough money from them to start up her savings again. Since her parents had died, she'd only made enough money to get by. But now with her freelancing gigs picking up, she should be able to get ahead. Or at least try to.

Two coffees and a week-old box of chocolate-chip cookies later, Laina had stopped procrastinating long enough to begin finalising the details on her current two projects. The hours sped by after that and she sated her hunger by continuing to graze on the minimal food in her fridge as she worked.

It was sometime later when she hit 'send' on the email to the client, just as a knock sounded from the door. She stood from her stool in the kitchen and stopped when she saw the deep orange glow that came in from the patio doors. It was late in the afternoon already. *How long was I working for?* The knocking came again, and she made her way over to the door to look through the peephole.

"Max," she said, opening the door.

"Hey, Laina," he said with a smile. Like usual, his hair was perfectly combed and spiked upwards. He was clean shaven and looking very refreshed in his black jeans, white shirt, and grey overcoat...and he was holding a box of pizza. Laina's stomach took that moment to rumble, reminding her she'd lived off chocolate cookies and coffee all day. He shrugged. "Just a hunch, but I figured you could use some food. Pizza?"

She sighed. "That would be amazing."

A slow smile spread out across his lips. "Let's eat," he said, walking into the room. "I got your favourite, margherita."

Laina's mouth watered as she closed the door. "You know me so well," she said on a sigh.

When she turned around, his smile had widened and there seemed to be an intensity there she hadn't recognised before.

"I do," he replied. Why did his voice sound husky? Max abruptly cleared his throat and seemed to snap out of wherever he had disappeared to in his head. What was the matter with him tonight?

"So," he started, breaking the awkward silence. "Uh, did you see the news?"

Max took off his overcoat and laid it down on the arm rest of the lounge. Whenever they had pizza, it was the same routine, they would sit on the floor with the pizza box between them as they shared the meal. And tonight was no different.

"They found body parts and bodies in that parkland near where we were last night. It looked like someone had tried to set fire to them too as there were scorch marks all over the grass. And the ones that were...intact...had those puncture wounds again." *That* made Laina stop mid-bite of her pizza as he continued. "I bet that creepy guy we saw last night had something to do with it." He shook his head and reached for the pizza. "Maybe we should report him."

Laina forced herself to take another bite and swallow. "Creepy guy?"

"Yeah, the one you were talking to last night. Maybe he was the one who did it." His eyes widened as he turned to her. "We could have been killed!"

You have no idea how right you are, she thought but instead she rolled her eyes. *Wait.* Could Max have been right? Could Ryon have killed those people? He didn't seem like a murderer...but then again, what the hell did she know? She didn't know anything about him.

"Anyway," Max said, folding his hands on his lap. "Listen..." he began to fidget, looking suddenly nervous. "I know you've had a hard six months, so I hope this isn't coming on too strong..."

Laina frowned and put down her half-eaten slice of pizza, unsure where this was going.

Max continued, "but I wanted to ask you..." He looked up at her in a way that she'd seen before but never recognised until this moment. *No.* "You're a beautiful woman..." he let the words linger before he fidgeted some more.

No. No. Don't make things awkward, Max. Don't do it. Max was a catch—there was no doubt about that. But there was no spark, no firework, no *chemistry* between them. He was her best friend, and he was so far in her friend-zone that he was practically her brother.

"I...ah...was wondering..." he ran a hand through his hair and dropped his gaze.

"Tea!" Laina suddenly announced, pulling herself up to stand. *Tea? Seriously, Laina?* "Would you like some tea?"

"Oh," Max hesitated, confused for a moment before he said, "um...sure, I guess."

Laina held back the sigh of relief as she made her way over to the kitchen. The last thing she wanted was yet another cup of tea, but she had to do something to stop those words from coming out. She needed to stop him from saying something that would be irreversible and would undeniably destroy the one friendship that was so important to her. What the hell was he thinking? They'd known each other a few years now, but she'd never given him the impression that she liked him in that way...had she?

She prepared two cups and then stared at the kettle as it boiled, losing herself in those liquid bubbles as they danced around and bumped into each other inside the clear glass. Her chaotic mind was just like those bubbles: her thoughts, bouncing around and taking turns to boil up to the surface before another one took over. Her parents' death, the alley, vampires, Ryon, the bodies in the parkland...and now Max. It was all *too much*.

When the light went off to signal the water was boiled, she poured the steaming hot water into the first cup, then the second cup...and then something caught her eye through the window beside her.

She stopped mid-pour and squinted out the large window that sat above the sink, realising that with Max's arrival she'd neglected to close all the blinds and curtains around the apartment. It was already dark and with the light on in the kitchen, it made the outdoors even darker—and harder to see. Being on the second floor and a corner apartment block, she had a wide-angle view of the nearby park and adjoining streets. Whilst her kitchen and bedroom windows looked out onto the park, her living room patio faced the street. Her heart raced as she looked into the night at the park across the road that was lined with trees. Was something there? She squinted, thinking she may have seen movement—

Her eyes adjusted to the darkness, and she could see a large figure standing at the edge of the park. A familiar, tall, and masculine figure that seemed to be looking straight at her with eyes that appeared to glow with gold. *Could it be him? How... how?* Her mind immediately ran through all the logical reasons of how it was not possible that Ryon—the vampire—was now standing across the road from her apartment, looking up into her kitchen window. But...but those eyes. They were *his* eyes. And why wasn't she afraid?

A hand suddenly reached out from behind her. She let out

a scream and jumped, forgetting all about the kettle she was still holding. Max cried out in pain as he yanked back his hand —the same hand that Laina had just unintentionally poured boiling hot water all over.

"Oh my God!" Laina hastily put the kettle down and reached for Max's hand. "We need to get it under cold water!" Bouncing around on his feet, Max continued to let out a string of curses as he reluctantly let Laina take his hand. "Oh God, I'm so sorry. I'm so, *so* sorry."

"It's fine," Max lied through clenched teeth as she placed his hand in the sink and began to run the cold water.

Her eyes darted out the window, hating herself for being more concerned about the figure outside than her best friend's new injury—that *she* had inflicted on him. But he was gone. *Had she imagined the whole thing?*

Max's hiss brought her attention back to his hand as the water touched his skin. *Shit.* The back of his entire hand was already welting up with angry red blisters. She'd given him third-degree burns...and cold water wasn't going to cut it. "We need to get you to the hospital."

CHAPTER SEVEN

"You need to get to the hospital," Fynn said urgently into the phone.

"Why? What's going on?" Ryon demanded, his gaze locked on the window of Laina's apartment. Thanks to Malik, he'd obtained her address and now stood across the road, looking at—going by the faucet that he could see just inside—her kitchen. The light was on so she must have been home, but he had yet to see her in the last five minutes he'd been standing here.

When Ryon heard Malik and the others return last night from their outing, he'd gone directly to ask him about finding Laina's address. Ryon had been grateful that Malik hadn't asked too many questions and the whole thing had taken all of two minutes. He'd fought the urge to fade directly to her apartment then and there and managed to get some shut eye instead. When he woke, he'd showered and had some unsatisfying human blood from the manor's freezer stash. As soon as the last ray of sunlight disappeared beyond the horizon, Ryon had faded here as soon as he could.

But now that he was here...he was second guessing why he'd come in the first place. *To wipe her memory. I'm here to wipe her memory*, he reminded himself. Only...he wasn't sure if he really wanted to.

He kind of liked the idea that he had a permanent home inside her memory bank.

"Hello? Ryon? Are you there, man?" Fynn's voice dragged Ryon's mind back to the present.

"Uh. Yeah. Yep. I'm here...sorry, you cut out. What did you say?"

Fynn must have changed the position of his phone as Ryon heard shuffling and then Fynn's voice suddenly a lot closer. "We've got an emergency at Ladwick hospital. Soran's pulling everyone in."

Fuck. He glanced away from the window as the seriousness of the situation sunk in. "What's going on?"

"No idea. All I know is that it's bad," Fynn answered. "I'm on my way now. Get there as soon as you can." Ryon heard the click as the call disconnected and put the phone back in his pocket. With one last glance up—

Laina's face suddenly appeared in the window. She was looking down at something in front of her. Her long brown hair was tied up in a bun above her head and she wore a black jumper...and that was all he could see from where he stood. She looked lost in thought, and he had a sudden urge to forget about whatever was going down in the hospital and stand here watching her for the rest of the night.

She was...beautiful. He'd known it last night but seeing her again just reaffirmed it. Those green eyes lifted from whatever it was she was looking at, and, as if knowing exactly where he was in the darkness, she looked directly at him. He knew his

48

eyes were glowing when her own widened and locked on his, sending a wave of emotion through him he'd never felt before. He felt like he *wanted* her, and not just for her blood—which was ludicrous because she was a human. And he'd never wanted a human in that way before.

Ryon knew he didn't have time to wipe her memory right now. He had to leave and get to the hospital, but his body refused to move. Her eyes had frozen him in place as sure as if she was the one who had the ability to mind control. Movement behind her caught his attention. Ryon's fangs elongated instantly, and a growl escaped his throat as he recognised the man behind her as the one from the alley. Her...*boyfriend.*

His fists tightened at the thought, and he felt the sharp sting of his nails digging into his palm. Why was he acting like this? Why did he care about the human at all? *Dammit!* He needed to get his shit together and focus on fading out of here. It took Ryon a few attempts to finally calm down enough to fade, and eventually, he was able to transport himself across to the hospital.

When Ryon appeared in the shadows beside the frosted double door glass entrance to the Ladwick hospital, he knew something was wrong. The lights were on inside, but it was eerily quiet—too quiet. There were no injured humans rushing inside, no concerned family members waiting outside —there was no one, despite the number of cars in the adjacent carpark.

As soon as he pushed open the doors—surprised to find them unlocked—the scent of human blood suddenly struck him.

His fangs descended in a rush, and he had to reach out for the wall to steady himself. Reining in his blood lust, he glanced around the reception area, a place usually hustling and bustling with humans. But it was empty. *Where is everyone?*

Cautiously, Ryon glanced down the many hallways, only to see more of nothing and no one. He heard the entrance door open, catching Fynn's scent before he turned around.

"Where the hell is everyone?" Fynn asked.

"No idea, but it smells like a massacre in here," Ryon replied. "I think we better lock those doors until we find out, though."

Fynn gave a nod of agreement and locked the double door entrance as Ryon made his way behind the reception desk counter. "The computers are still on," he observed. He glanced around at the half-full mugs, the bottles of water, the pens dropped haphazardly by the keyboards and the office chairs pushed back from the desks. But no blood. "It looks like they've just dropped everything and left."

"Or they were compelled to," Fynn replied.

The sound of a door exploding open had them glancing at a fire exit door at the opposite end of the reception. A human woman stumbled out wearing light blue scrubs. Her hair was pulled back in a ponytail which did nothing to conceal the large laceration at her neck that was bleeding down onto the collar of her uniform. She looked frantically around the empty reception area before bolting towards the front doors, completely oblivious to the two large males nearby.

"Whoa there, sweetheart," Fynn said, casually stepping in front of her before she could reach the doors. "What's going on?"

The woman mumbled incoherently as her wide eyes danced around the room, never focusing on any one thing. *She's in shock.* Fynn reached out and took hold of the woman's face, looking into her eyes. "You're going to find something to apply pressure to that wound on your neck, and then you're going to lock yourself in an empty room until someone comes to get you. Nod your head if you understand." Fynn released her face, and she nodded before turning and walking calmly down one of the many hallways.

"Upstairs," Fynn said decidedly, snapping Ryon out of his thoughts.

Together, they sped for the fire exit the woman had come out of. Once they pushed open the heavy door, the sound of screams, yells, and scuffles echoed down the stairwell. Ryon let out a curse as he began to take two steps at a time, with Fynn right behind him.

When they reached the first floor, Ryon didn't hesitate. He kicked open the door and into...*chaos*. Fynn let out a string of obscenities from beside him, and together they took in the scene.

Humans and pools of stained blood lined the left-hand side of the hallway they had entered. Some humans huddled in corners crying. Others were in such a state of shock they appeared almost comatose. Or maybe they were dead—who knew? Ryon could hear so many different heartbeats that it was hard to tell who they were coming from. More yelling, hissing, and scuffling came from somewhere down the hallway, and as he moved forward, he saw scattered bodies. There were women. There were men. Some were wearing blue scrubs; some wore white patient gowns—but *all* of them had gaping wounds at their throats.

"Reds," Fynn said from behind him. "It has to be Reds."

The sound of yelling grew louder, and Soran's familiar voice rang out. A ripple of fear started in Ryon's stomach and slowly crept towards his chest. *This is not good.* A group of Reds losing control in a human hospital was going to attract too much attention. Way too much attention. It would be all over the news by morning if they didn't get it under control.

Fynn started running down the hallway, and Ryon followed suit. They passed numerous still-bleeding dead bodies and injured humans that looked up at them with eyes that were glazed over. *Compulsion.* The humans that remained alive had been compelled to stay put.

"Stop!" Soran's voice echoed from somewhere close by, but as they reached the first-floor reception desk, they stopped short. Three human bodies were thrown over the desk, blood pooling at the top of it and trickling down to the floor. Ryon took that moment to reach behind and unsheathe the sword from his back, waiting as Fynn did the same. Three hallways branched off from the reception area, but he already knew which one he was headed for. If Soran's voice didn't give it away, the Reds scent easily did.

"Let them go!" he heard Soran shout. And then Ryon ran. He knew Fynn was on his heels as they turned the corner and saw the Shadows—all of them—forming a line behind Soran as he held his own sword out in front of him. Ryon halted, his brows drawn together as he took in his fellow Shadows— Xavier, Malik, Rune, Darick, Damien and Kove. They all stood with their swords unsheathed by their sides—but where was Zane?

"You can't stop us. Not anymore," a male voice said with a hiss.

Ryon followed Soran's line of sight to see ten or more Reds standing in front of an open lift. Their red eyes were frenzied with blood lust, their mouths were covered in dark crimson, their fangs bared, and they held humans in front of them as shields as they backed up into the lift.

"Mother *fuckers*!" Soran muttered as he stalked forward, searching for a way to use his sword without causing any collateral damage. Killing humans was against the rules, but they'd have a much bigger problem on their hands if the Reds escaped.

"Just kill them!" Xavier called out.

"You know I can't. It's too risky," Soran replied through gritted teeth, without taking his eyes off the Reds.

"Zane?" Damien called out. "Zane, what the fuck are you doing?"

Zane had come out of one of the rooms to stand before the group of Reds, facing his fellow Shadow members. His weapon of choice—a bow and arrow—was slung over his shoulder like usual. His short blond hair was slicked back, but his eyes...Ryon bit back a curse as he noticed Zane's eyes were a deep, scarlet red—a contrast to their usual blue colour. *Lost. He's lost.*

Zane pulled back his lips, exposing his elongated fangs. "Times are changing." His voice was a deep growl that was tinged with fury. "This world no longer belongs to the humans," he said, stepping back into the lift and joining the Reds. "It is *ours*, and we are taking it *back*."

"Fuck. Fuck. Fuck!" Soran shouted.

Ryon watched helplessly as Soran ran forward, just as the doors closed.

CHAPTER EIGHT

"Come on, Laina, this is ridiculous. I'm fine! I just need to put some ice on it," Max said from the passenger seat of Laina's car.

She pulled into the carpark and turned off the car before turning to glare at him. "You have no skin on the back of your hand. I'd say it's going to take more than some ice and a band aid, Max."

Max rolled his eyes and Laina got out of the car, walking around the front to open the door for Max. When she noticed he was struggling to unbuckle his seat belt with one hand, she leaned over him and reached around to find the button. She managed to release it but when she made to move back, Max held her arm in place.

"Laina..." he whispered, his face mere inches from hers. Every muscle in Laina's body tensed. *Not again. Not now.*

"Max," she started, not knowing how to word what she was trying to say...and not sure if now was the right time.

Max shook his head. "Please, just hear me out." Laina glanced down when Max let go of her arm, but her relief was short lived when he started to run his fingertips up and down the inside of her elbow.

"What's going on? I need a doctor!"

"Hey! Let us in!"

The sound of angry voices had Laina jerking back out of the car and away from Max's reach to glance across the road to the entrance of the hospital. It looked like it was…closed? And those voices belonged to the number of angry people who were banging on the double door entrance demanding to be let in.

"Is it closed?" Max asked, getting out of the car. "I didn't know hospitals could close."

"Neither did I," she replied, relieved at the sudden change in conversation. She closed the door after him as they both made their way over to the crowd. There was no sign on the hospital door and from what she could see through the frosted glass, no one was moving about inside, despite the lights being on.

"See? This is just another reason to turn around and go back home," Max said.

Laina needed to find an excuse not to go back to her place. Or even back to the car with Max. She didn't want to give him another opportunity to take the conversation to where he wanted it to go. She didn't need this right now. And she didn't want to lose what they had. Her friendship with Max was special to her, it was important to her, and she didn't want to change that and make things awkward.

"Maybe they just opened up another entrance around the back and no one's noticed," Laina said, gesturing for Max to follow her around the side of the building.

Max sighed loudly but joined her as they made their way

down the side of the hospital. The crowd of people were too busy banging on the door and yelling amongst themselves to notice the pair as they walked further down to the far end of the building.

"No entrance, let's go," Max said.

Laina shot Max a glare before she pointed at the double metallic doors. "There's a lift over there."

Max attempted to cross his arms over his chest, only to hiss in pain at his burned hand. "Yeah, the sign says staff-only, and we're not staff," he gritted out.

"I'm calling the lift."

Max sighed again. "Laina, this is crazy."

As soon as Laina pressed the button, the doors to the lift opened. "Huh. What do you know? Come on. I'm sure it's just that the front doors have malfunctioned, and the staff haven't put up the signs directing people this way up." She stepped inside the lift and Max reluctantly joined her. "Let's try the first floor." Laina pressed the button and after a short ride, the doors opened on an empty hallway.

"That's strange." Laina said, frowning as she stepped out of the lift. "Where is everyone?"

"Oh, *that's* what's strange?" Max retorted as he joined her. "Not the part about the hospital being closed for the first time, in like, ever?"

Laina ignored Max's comment as they made their way to the end of the hallway. She thought she could hear voices but as she walked past each patient room, she couldn't see anyone inside. But then her gaze landed on a small red puddle on the floor, and she froze. *Is that blood?* She stepped closer to inspect it, but her attention was drawn to the nearby reception desk at the end of the hallway...which had the same red substance smeared across it.

Her stomach twisted with dread as she began to realise something more sinister than just a malfunctioning front door was going on. "Maybe we should get out of here," she whispered.

As if Max hadn't heard her at all, he stepped forward and let out a choking sound. His breath hitched, and she stepped forward to see what he was looking at...

Oh my God. There were bodies...*everywhere.* Men, women, doctors, nurses, patients...all scattered down the hallway. Some were sitting up, some lying down, some had their eyes open... but *all* of them had puncture wounds at their throat. *Oh God.* Just like her parents. Just like the bodies that had been showing up overnight. *Vampires. There were vampires here.* Laina wanted to scream but there was no air left in her lungs as her wide eyes darted from body to body.

"I..." Max's shaky voice had her glancing over at him. Max was swaying slightly on his feet, the colour in his skin drained as Laina recalled the way blood made him queasy.

Pushing aside her own fear and panic, she jumped in front of him and shook his shoulders. "Max, stay with me. Don't you faint on me!" *Not now, damn it!* She knew what he was like with the sight of blood but now was *not* the time! Max didn't even seem to notice Laina as he continued to stare off into the distance behind her.

"What do we have here?"

The male voice had her swinging around just as a tall, slim man came around the corner. He was dressed casually in dark jeans and a grey shirt. He was pale, with short blond hair, and his eyes...his eyes were *red*. The breath caught in her throat, and she fought back the urge to run when she heard the sound of Max's body hitting the floor behind her. She couldn't run now. She couldn't leave Max here. *Dammit! Shit. Shit. Shit.*

"Well, didn't you pick the wrong night to visit the hospital," he said with a chuckle. And that was when she saw it. The *fangs.*

She gasped, terror coursing its way through her body as he stalked closer as if he were a lion and she, an injured gazelle. She knew it. *Vampires.* She tried to back up, but Max's body prevented her from moving any further.

So, she opened her mouth and did the only thing she *could* do. She screamed.

CHAPTER NINE

L aina. It was *Laina*. Ryon knew it was her down to the depths of his bones. He had no idea *how* he knew it, but instinct told him she was somewhere in the hospital...and that scream belonged to her.

Soran had gone back to the manor to contact the King which left the rest of the Shadows to wipe the minds of those alive and dispose of the bodies of the dead—which was easy enough to do with the morgue downstairs. Ryon glanced over his shoulder at where Kove and Fynn had been checking each human for a pulse. But they had stopped what they were doing, their heads turned in the direction of the scream. They'd heard it too. And considering all humans in this facility were either dead, or compelled to stay still and be quiet, it wouldn't be long until someone found her.

And that same instinct of his told him to get there first.

Without another thought, he closed his eyes and faded in the direction of her scream until he caught her scent. He appeared at the entrance to a hallway and tensed as he took in the scene. A Red was standing with his back to Ryon as he approached a frightened Laina.

Before Ryon considered what he was doing, he was moving. And just as the Red reached Laina, Ryon lunged— too fast for the human eye—and slammed sideways into him, taking him to the ground. He heard Laina gasp, but he couldn't focus on that now.

The Red hissed and sneered as he rolled around, fighting Ryon's hold and struggling to get the upper hand. But Ryon was stronger. In one swift move, he pinned the Red on his back as he pressed his knees into the Red's chest.

"Want her for yourself, do you?" the Red relinquished with a smirk. Ryon lifted his arm and unsheathed the sword at his back, placing it to the Red's throat. Unconcerned, the Red added, "That's cool. We can share."

Pure rage shot through Ryon at the words, and he let out a hiss as he swung the sword around in one hand, repositioning it as he plunged it down into the Red's skull.

Panting, Ryon pulled his sword back and wiped it on the Red's clothes, realising he'd have to wipe Laina's memory not only from last night but tonight too. Wiping a human's memory was like reaching for a specific apple at the bottom of a barrel full of apples. Doing it once was easy enough, but doing it twice meant having to shuffle all those other apples aside to find the right one, potentially causing permanent damage. And for some reason, Ryon cared about Laina's apples.

Ryon sheathed his sword once more as he heard Laina's voice behind him. "Max?"

He turned to face Laina, aware that any second now the other Shadows would appear if they heard voices and didn't think Ryon was taking care of the human who screamed. Whatever he was going to do, he needed to do it *fast*.

Laina was kneeling beside *Max*, who, by the sound of his heartbeat was only unconscious not dead. Ryon stepped forward, immediately recognising the man as the one from the alley...and from her apartment earlier. *Her boyfriend*, Ryon reminded himself as he pushed aside those now familiar feelings of jealousy. What the *fuck* was wrong with him?

"You need to hide," Ryon gritted out in a low voice. *Until I can come back and wipe your memory.*

Laina glanced up briefly before shaking her head and looking back down at Max. "I can't leave him."

Ryon let out a curse. He didn't have time for this. He walked over and knelt beside Max, picking him up and earning a gasp from Laina. "In there," he said, nodding to the patient room he'd noticed at the opposite end of the hallway. Laina followed him silently as Ryon kicked open the door, grateful to find it empty and unlocked. He fought the urge to drop Max on the bed but instead, he lay him down gently, and walked over to the door to test the lock.

Laina swung around to face him, her eyes wide. "What... what are you doing?"

"Relax," he replied flatly, facing her. "I have no plans to kill you, but..." *Fuck. Why was he hesitating?* He turned away from her and ran a hand through his hair, feeling the tug of those scars on his hand again as frustration roiled through him. *Erase her memories. Erase yourself from her memories.*

"But what?" Laina asked softly.

He hesitated before turning to face her. "But...I need to make you forget."

Laina's brows dropped on a frown before her eyes

widened slightly at the realisation. "I don't want to forget," she said, barely louder than a whisper. "Please don't make me forget. I won't tell anyone, I promise."

Ryon halted as her words triggered something inside of him that made him want to take it all back. Her gentle voice called to him, pleaded with him, and he found himself unable to say no to her. What sorcery was this? He was the one with the ability to mind control, yet she seemed to be able to pull his strings and play with his emotions and make him do things he'd never even considered doing before. He needed to wipe her memories and move on already.

At Ryon's silence, Laina tried again. "Please," she stepped forward. He watched as she swallowed hard as if attempting to make her voice stronger...and didn't that just play with his emotions even more. "I need to remember that you...that you exist. That your kind exists. I...I've had too many questions that have been answered by knowing...knowing that *vampires* exist." She inhaled. "Please don't take that away."

Fuck. Ryon pursed his lips and turned from her. *Fuck. Fuck. Fuck.* He needed to get away from her and think on this. Not to mention the others were probably looking for him by now.

Facing her once more, he said, "I need to go. Lock this door after me and I'll come back when it's safe." He turned for the door but stopped when he heard Laina's voice.

"Wait!" He swung around and met those green eyes again. He had a fleeting thought that he could stand here and look into them forever, but then he shook his head and wiped the thought from his mind.

"W-when you come back, are you going to make me forget?" she asked.

Before Ryon knew what he was doing, he strode up to her. His body moved so effortlessly, so easily, towards her as if it were the most natural thing in the world. As if their bodies were two sides of a magnet being drawn together.

He reached her, standing so close that she needed to crane her neck up to look at him. He half expected her to step back, but she didn't. He could still see the fear in her eyes, but she lifted her chin and stood her ground, and for some reason he felt a flicker of pride for this little human in front of him. After what she'd seen last night and tonight, and the fear that she must have been feeling, she was standing up for herself. Suddenly he found himself wondering what had happened to make her such a strong person underneath all that fear.

And then her scent hit him. The delectable scent that made him want to throw all inhibitions aside and feed from her and *fuck* her at the same time—something he'd never even contemplated before. This little human woman was making him question...everything. It was dangerous. And it was in that moment that he recognised what he needed to do.

CHAPTER TEN

Laina spent the next ten minutes pacing around the room and checking on Max while deliberating her next move. Ryon could come back at any minute...to wipe her memories. Deep down, she would love nothing more than to forget about last night and the horrors she'd seen already tonight but none of that would take away the fact that vampires existed. And she wanted to remember that. She *needed* to remember that. For the sake of her parents.

Max's hand was blistered and red but other than that he would probably wake up soon. Laina had pulled out her phone more than once, readying to call her sister, but what would she say? *'Can you come and pick me up from the hospital? Max is unconscious and I've locked myself in a room to avoid the vampires running riot through the wards. Oh, and uh...mind the bodies.'*

Brynn would either scream at her for not telling her about vampires sooner or tell her she was crazy and hang up. But what if Brynn was already on her way to the hospital, anyway? There weren't *that* many police officers in Ladwick and when word spread about this? They'd all be called. Laina's stomach twisted in knots at the thought of losing Brynn the same way she lost her parents. No. *No.* She had to call her. She had to warn her. With a glance back at the still-sleeping Max, she scrolled through her contacts to find Brynn.

"Laina?" Brynn asked, answering after the first ring as sirens echoed in the background.

"Yeah, it's me," Laina replied in a whisper.

"Why are you whispering? Where are you?"

"Listen, I...I think something's going down at the hospital."

"How do you know that? Are you there? My *God* Laina, are you *in* the hospital?" Brynn demanded. "Tell me you're not in the hospital! We've been informed about a situation, but we don't know any more than that."

"I'm fine," Laina rushed out. "But yes, I'm in the hospital. In one of the rooms on the first floor. But...but..." How to tell Brynn about what was outside the room?

"I'm on my way now, the whole force is," Brynn said. "Wait where you are. I'll come and find you."

Brynn ended the call, and it took all of two seconds for Laina to decide that she wasn't going to wait around for her sister to find her. The sounds of the sirens in the background told Laina that Brynn was almost here, and she glanced back at Max once more. Laina could do it. If she hurried, she could get to Brynn and get help before Max woke up or Ryon came back.

"Stay there," she told Max needlessly as she put her phone in the back pocket of her jeans. She went to the door and when she couldn't hear anything on the other side, she cracked it open.

Her eyes raked over the hall just outside but there was nothing. She frowned, craning her neck further. No dead bodies, no blood, nothing. She was alone. But how? *How did they clean-up so fast? And where did all the bodies go?*

No time for wondering all of that now. She pushed open the door, closed it behind her and padded down the hallway back the way she came. She kept her back against the wall and slowly made her way to the lift again. She was about to press the call button when she noticed the fire escape stairwell to the left. *The fire stairs would be faster.*

Reaching the fire exit, she gently pushed on the metal bar, hoping it wouldn't make a sound and attract unwanted attention. The small clang as the door opened had Laina squeezing her eyes closed. When she heard nothing, she opened her eyes and let out a sigh of relief as she stepped forward.

"Hey Fynn, we missed one," a man called out, making every bone in Laina's body tense.

With one hand on the fire escape door, she glanced over her shoulder at the large man staring at her from the hallway. He had long dark hair that fell loosely to his shoulders, a beard that hung down past his chin, and he wore black leather pants and a black leather jacket with...*ribbed sleeves.* Just like Ryon. *Was he a vampire, too?*

She opened her mouth to say something, but all that came out was a scream when he suddenly appeared an arm's length away. The hairs on the back of her neck stood on end and a wave of panic rushed through her. His eyes were *glowing* the colour of molten lava.

Her hands began to sweat, her palm slipping from the door handle, causing it to swing back against her. She glanced down the stairwell. She could run but considering how fast the man—no, vampire—was, he could get to her before she reached the first step.

"Look at me," the man said. And to her horror, her neck turned without her willing it to until her eyes locked on his. What was happening? She tried to turn away from the vampire, but she couldn't. She was frozen in place, watching the man as if waiting for a command.

But none came.

Instead, a slight gust of wind brushed past her, causing the loose strands of hair that had fallen out of her bun to fly across her face and break her out of whatever trance she was in. Laina blinked a few times before she realised what had happened. Ryon was there. He'd...just...*appeared* and now pinned the other man up against the wall with an elbow to his neck. The sound of the police sirens echoed up the stairwell and with her back still holding the fire exit door open, she glanced down the dark stairs. *Were the police here already?*

"What the fuck are you doing, Ryon?" the man grated out as his hands came up to grip at Ryon's arm.

Laina froze. The man had called Ryon by name. They knew each other.

"She's going to get away, we need to—" The vampire's words were cut off by a choking sound when Ryon jabbed his elbow further into his neck. Laina let out a gasp, lifting her hand to her mouth to stifle the sound.

"She won't tell anyone," Ryon gritted out. She could see the muscle in his jaw ticking as he clenched his teeth together, straining to keep the vampire up against the wall. He sent a glance her way, and she noticed the colour of his brown eyes had now turned a fiery amber. The vampire against the wall was fighting Ryon's hold, but Ryon held firm, his eyes never leaving hers. She swallowed hard and jerkily nodded.

"She's a fucking liability!" The man said in a strained voice. "You do it, or I will!"

Ryon turned back to him. "You are not to touch her or talk to her, do you hear?"

He's protecting me. Again. For some stupid and ridiculous reason, butterflies began to flicker around inside Laina's stomach. Maybe all this chaos was messing with her notion of fear because butterflies were the last thing she should be feeling right now.

The man against the wall let out a hiss, and she saw two twin white fangs protrude from his mouth. She didn't stifle the gasp this time, but Ryon didn't even so much as flinch. His body was tight with tension. He merely lifted his other hand to reinforce the elbow at the vampire's neck.

And then those fiery eyes turned back to her. "Go!"

Laina wanted to move. *Really*, she did. But her legs didn't get the memo. Instead, she remained frozen in fear, watching as the two large vampires struggled.

"Don't you fucking do this, Ryon!" the vampire choked out.

"*Go!*" Ryon roared at her.

And this time, as if his words were a direct order that she couldn't defy, she ran.

CHAPTER ELEVEN

Ryon woke to the sound of a deafening bang. Sitting up, he glanced around his darkened bedroom and was relieved to see the outside shutters and heavy drapes still in place protecting him from the outside sun. Deciding he must have imagined the noise, he lay back down and rolled onto his side when he heard a female's scream. He knew that voice.

He didn't so much jump out of bed as stumble his way out in a tangle of bedsheets. Making his way to the bedroom door, he yanked it open and felt his heart turn to concrete in his chest. The single most important person in his life, his mother, was dragged kicking and screaming out of her bedroom by two males double her size, wearing black robes.

"What are you doing? Let her go!" Ryon yelled, rushing forward to tug at one of the male's arms to no avail. He had no idea who these males were or what they wanted with his mother, but he wasn't about to let them take her away without a fight. The male shrugged Ryon off with little to no effort before dragging his mother down the hallway of their little cottage and into the living room, where more males in black robes were waiting.

In a desperate attempt to plead with the group, Ryon hastily went over to the male in the red robe with some sort of crest on the shoulder and fell to his feet. This had to be their leader. "Please. Please. Please let her go. She hasn't done anything wrong. We haven't done anything wrong. Please." He was sobbing now, but he was helpless to stop the tears from falling.

The echo of a male's laughter filled the room before that deep, gritty voice of the male in the red robe spoke. "Begging, boy? How pathetic." The male kicked Ryon, and he fell on his backside.

Ryon's sobbing grew louder, and he moved forward on his knees over the peeling vinyl of the floor that they couldn't afford to fix. He shuffled until he reached the flowing red material of the male's robe. Clutching it tightly in his hand, he continued to plead. "Take me instead! Please, take me instead!"

"No, Ryon! No!" His mother's yell had him turning around to face her. Her golden eyes locked on his with sorrow and acceptance, and deep down, he knew this was the last time he'd ever meet that gaze. "You're better than this!" she cried out as she was shoved over to the front door.

No. No. No. Ryon's realisation had him releasing the red robe to get to his feet. *No!*

"You're better than this!" she screamed louder as someone opened the front door. The blinding sunlight streamed into the room, had everyone hissing and falling back. Everyone except the two males holding his mother. *NO!*

"You're better than *him*!" he heard his mother's straining

voice, but he'd closed his eyes against the glare of the sunlight. The heat was already intense, and he was on the other side of the room while his mother...

Ryon opened his eyes and lifted a hand to shield his vision as he witnessed the two males in black robes push her outside and into the direct sun.

NOOOO! Ryon let his hand fall, his eyes burning against the glare as he watched his mother stumble onto the grass outside, the exposed skin on her face and arms peeling away as smoke appeared around her. *She's burning. She's burning!*

Despite the agony she must have been feeling, his mother pushed herself up to stand and turned around to face him. "I love you," she mouthed before she threw her head back, her arms out, and surrendered to the sun.

Ryon screamed so loud his own ears rang in response, and then he was moving. He sprinted for the door, tears streaming down his face and the echo of his own scream in his ears. He reached out past the threshold, exposing his hand and wrist to the blistering sunlight just as the two males by the door caught him around the chest, stopping him from going any further.

He fought their hold, but it was all for nothing. It was too late. His mother was nothing more than a dusting of ash being taken away on the slight gust of wind passing by.

Ryon fell back inside as the males closed the door. His hand and wrist burned as if they were on fire, but the pain didn't even come close to the suffering he felt on the inside. He was sure there was a gaping hole in the middle of his chest where his heart should have been. Had he been shot? Had someone ripped out his heart?

He lifted his hand to his chest but felt nothing other than the thin fabric of his sleepwear. He glanced down just to make sure, and that's when he noticed his hand. The nerve endings in his arm took that moment to communicate the excruciating agony to his brain. His hand was...burned. The skin along the back of his hand and up to his wrist was already healing from the poisonous kiss of the sun. The flesh there now distorted and raised in a permanent scar that, just like the hollow ache in his chest, would never go away.

"Fuck!" Ryon cried out as he sprung up in bed, his hand burning like it was on fire. Gritting his teeth against the pain, he leaned over and turned on his bedside light. He quickly glanced around the room and was relieved to find the familiar layout of his bedroom in the manor, not a small cottage. He lifted his hand up, the pain now only a dull ache yet there were no new injuries or wounds on his flesh.

What the hell was that? Vampires could dream...but he'd never had a dream like that before. That felt so vivid. So...*real*.

He lay back on the bed with a sigh and ran his scarred hand through his hair. He lifted it in front of him, turning it over and inspecting the burn that ran up his wrist. With no memory of life as a human, he never knew what had caused the disfiguration. It *had* to have happened before his transition because as a vampire, not only would he have remembered the incident, but he would also have healed.

Frankly, he never thought too much about it, but after that dream...He ran a fingertip over the raised flesh and couldn't help but wonder what *had* happened. Had he placed his hand in boiling water as a child? Had he run into a burning building to save someone? What had his life been like as a human? It was pointless wondering, however. None of those questions would be answered. During the transition process, the King would have all forms of human identification removed and destroyed so to not cause confusion since vampires couldn't remember their lives as humans—or at least that's what Soran had explained to him a long time ago.

Ryon put that dream down to his wild imagination and rolled over to unplug his phone from the charger on his bedside table. The clock on the home screen told him it was almost dark and time to get up for the night. After a quick shower, he put on a new pair of jeans, a grey t-shirt, and his leather jacket, before sheathing his sword. He wasn't sure if anyone would be on patrol after what went down in the hospital last night, but he wanted to be prepared just in case.

Leaving his room, he made his way down the long hallway, past all the other closed bedrooms, and then down to the first floor. He wasn't surprised that the halls were empty. After last night, a veil of sadness had fallen over the manor. With the Reds out on the streets and the humans at their mercy, soon word would spread far and wide about the existence of vampires, and their entire species would be under threat.

And then there was Zane.

Ryon had to admit, he wasn't surprised that Zane had jumped ship seeing as he hated humans so much, but it didn't make any of this easier. Zane had become one of The Shadows. He was their colleague, and their friend. And now, a *Red*.

He scrubbed a hand over his face as he walked further down the corridor. The first signs of hunger were creeping in, and Ryon planned to head to the kitchen for a blood bag to satiate his thirst. He stopped short when he heard a female voice coming from the drawing room. Frowning, he made his way closer until he could scent his friends inside and realised the female voice was the TV.

"There has been no new activity here at the Ladwick Hospital. It remains closed for investigations, but we will continue to bring you updates as we receive them. Back to you at the Studio, Brian."

Ryon stepped into the room and saw Fynn, Xavier, Malik, Rune, and the two brothers—Damien and Darick—scattered on the various armchairs and lounges in the room with their eyes glued to the TV. No sign of Kove, however.

"Any word from Zane?" he asked. Malik 'shushed' him, but when the brothers looked up at him, their expressions told him enough. After all, they were closest to Zane in the manor.

Fynn stood and joined him at the doorway. "No word from Zane," Fynn confirmed before gesturing to the TV. "But check it out. They've been reporting on it for hours."

Ryon glanced over at the screen just as a middle-aged man spoke up from behind a studio desk. "Thanks for the update, Kim. As the events from last night continue to unfold, let's recap what we know so far..." The man turned to a large screen behind him as CCTV footage began to show men and women outside the hospital banging on the closed doors and yelling to be let in.

"At nine p.m. last night, the only Hospital in Ladwick closed its doors, preventing sick and injured citizens from getting the urgent care they required. At ten p.m., police were made aware of the unusual activity, and by ten-thirty, they entered the building by force. But here's where it gets interesting. At eleven p.m., police escorted at least one hundred doctors, nurses, and patients—each with varying degrees of injuries—out of the building." Ryon watched as the screen behind the man showed humans wearing scrubs, plain clothes, and patient gowns walking out of the hospital in a zombie-like state. "But in a mysterious turn of events," the man continued, "none of these witnesses can recall anything from the two hours prior. Not *one* of those people can explain why the doors were locked, how they got their injuries, or what had happened. It is being reported that they were all found in groups inside patient rooms, but none of them can remember how they got there. Very bizarre indeed."

The screen continued to show the humans piling out of the hospital, and Ryon's gaze drifted to the far left-hand side of the footage. *Is that...Laina?* He straightened and took a step closer to the TV as—*yes, definitely Laina*—ran through the crowd of on-lookers and straight for a woman in a police uniform, embracing her. Did they know each other? He watched, his chest tightening with some kind of emotion as Laina stepped back from the woman and wiped her eyes. *Crying.* She'd been crying. Of course, she'd been crying after everything she'd witnessed inside of that hospital.

He *should* have wiped her memory. He should have stopped her from running away and made her forget. But when he saw Kove approach her, something clicked inside of him and his need to protect Laina surged forward, making him act without thought. But did he regret his actions? He wasn't so sure...She'd pleaded with him to let her keep her memories. She all but *begged* him to and even though he had tried to maintain his reserve, he probably would have run head-long into the sun if that's what she'd asked of him.

Clearing his throat, Ryon turned to Fynn. "Who's on rotation tonight? I haven't seen an update from Soran, but after last night I'm assuming we're all needed out on the field to clean-up after the Reds."

Fynn shook his head. "Soran's pulled everyone off until we work out what's going on. He left a few hours ago to go visit the King directly."

"And where's Kove?" Ryon asked hesitantly. Had Kove told the others about what happened with Laina?

"He was here watching the footage with me earlier but then he just up and left," Fynn answered with a shrug.

"Oh, yeah!" Malik announced, looking over at them from the lounge. "Funny story. Kove came to find me and asked me to track down that woman." He gestured to the screen and the breath caught in Ryon's throat as he followed the pointed direction to...*Laina*. "And you wouldn't believe it, turns out that's the same woman *you* asked me to find only yesterday. I told him I'd already given you her address, but he wanted it anyway."

"When did he leave?" Ryon gritted out.

"About ten minutes ago." It was Fynn that answered, his brows lowered in confusion. "What's going on?"

Ryon didn't respond. He turned and bolted at a dead run down the hallway for the front door. If he went straight to Laina's apartment, maybe he could intercept Kove before he got there. A wave of pure protective rage washed over him as he yanked open the front door and faded away, not bothering to close the door behind him.

CHAPTER TWELVE

"How's your hand?" Laina asked into the phone as she curled up tighter on the armchair.

"It's pretty good considering I was passed out for most of the painful part," Max replied with a snort. It was true. After passing out from the sight of blood...and, well, *bodies*...he had only woken up when paramedics had placed ammonia under his nose. And he could remember...nothing. *Thank God.*

Laina *almost* wished that she could forget everything she'd seen last night, but it would also mean forgetting the truth about vampires. And *Ryon*. For some stupid reason, she didn't want to forget him either. She never expected him to let her go...but he did. He'd let her go without wiping her memory...*again*. And it seemed he went against his own friend to do it. But why?

"...today?"

Max's voice broke Laina out of her train of thought. "Sorry? What did you say?"

"How did you go today? At the station? I know they

called in everyone who was at the hospital last night," Max said.

Yes. Yes, they did. Today, the Ladwick police station had been a revolving door of people, all coming in to be interviewed over what happened in the hospital last night. Most people were only interviewed for a short time given there was a two-hour window of nothing in their memory. Laina had been tempted to say something right there in her interview, to tell the officer everything and get it all off her chest, but then she had recalled what Ryon had done for her and what he'd asked of her. He didn't want her telling anyone about what she'd seen...and she owed him that. So instead, she'd claimed Max fainted from the pain, that she dragged him into a patient room and that was where they stayed until she heard the sirens and ran out to find her sister.

When Laina didn't respond to Max, he continued, "the cops agreed to let me come in during my lunch break at work so I wouldn't have to take time off. I don't think my boss would have been too pleased if I had to take leave on my first day."

Max's new job. How could I forget? "I'm so sorry, I haven't asked you how your new job's going!"

Max chuckled. "It's all good, nothing much to say so far. I'm learning a lot and everyone's nice and—oh! I meant to ask you, there's a Design Gala I've been invited to..."

Laina stopped listening to Max when she heard a knock at the door. She pulled back her phone to check the time—Eight p.m. Who was knocking at the door at this time of night? It obviously wasn't Max, and she was sure Brynn said she was on night shift again. *A neighbour?* With the phone still to her ear, she walked over to check the peep hole—no one there. *Must have imagined it.*

"...so, what do you say?"

"About what?"

"The Design Gala? Will you be my plus one?"

"Oh! Uh..." *Like a date?* The thought of giving Max another opportunity to talk about their relationship made her want to retch. Another knock sounded, and Laina's frown deepened. *That almost sounded like it came from the patio.* Without another thought, she said, "uh, sure, I'll come. Sounds amazing. Listen, someone's at the door, so I've got to go. I'll call you tomorrow."

Laina hung up the phone before Max could respond. She made her way over to the patio and pulled the curtains back enough to peek outside. Brown eyes flickered with gold as they met hers through the glass, making her breath hitch as panic coursed through her. She recognised those eyes. She recognised that long dark hair that now fell loosely over his shoulders and his thick beard that hung below his chin. And she recognised that black leather jacket that looked just like Ryon's. It was the man, the *vampire*, from last night. The one Ryon had saved her from.

She tried to step back, she tried to move, but she was frozen in place. She tried to look away, but her eyes were locked on his and she couldn't do anything about it.

"Open the door," he said in a deep, threatening voice. And without another thought, Laina's hands moved of their own accord, pulling back the curtain more and sliding the glass door open.

"Now, stand back and let me in."

Her eyes remained on his as she backed up so far that she

passed the lounge and armchair until she felt the wall at her back. She could feel her heart pounding against her chest as she watched on in horror, unable to stop him from entering her apartment and unsure what he would do once inside.

"Stay there," he said as he glanced around the apartment before turning back to her. "I don't know what's going on with Ryon, but he never should have let you leave the hospital like that." He took a step closer. "And now I have to clean-up his mess."

CHAPTER THIRTEEN

Appearing across the road from Laina's apartment, Ryon immediately looked up to her kitchen window to see that the lights were on. He ran across the quiet road, to the front entrance of her building and let out a curse when he scented Kove. He glanced up to Laina's patio as that protective rage increased tenfold when he noticed the heavy drapes were pulled back slightly and the glass sliding door open wide.

Without hesitation, Ryon faded just inside the glass door... and appeared directly behind Kove in what looked to be Laina's living room. He saw Laina over Kove's shoulder. She was standing against the far wall in loose striped pants and a thin white tank top as she looked directly at Kove with wide, glazed over eyes.

He was too late.

Like a shot, Ryon wrapped an arm around Kove's neck from behind, pulling him back. He heard Laina gasp as Kove grunted and tried to break free, but Ryon only locked him in tighter using his other arm.

"I'm getting really fucking tired of having your arm at my neck," Kove choked out.

With teeth clenched, Ryon replied, "then don't give me a reason to."

Kove snarled and jerked forward, the force sending Ryon over Kove's back and onto a rug that sat between an armchair and a lounge. Grateful that Laina didn't own a coffee table, Ryon was on his feet before Kove could come back at him. Or so he thought.

The tackle came from the side. Ryon grunted when he felt the *snap* of a few ribs as Kove took him down to the ground. Kove's weight was on his back in an instant, his cheek pressed hard into the rug.

Fighting Kove's hold, Ryon ignored the screaming pain from his ribs and managed to overthrow his former friend, rolling so he was now the one on top with Kove's back planted firmly on the floor. Ryon gripped Kove's shirt with one hand, balled his other hand into a fist and thrust it into Kove's face. Ryon felt a rush of satisfaction when he heard the snap of Kove's nose before blood began to trickle out.

Kove snarled and threw his first back, readying to punch. Ryon braced himself, prepared to move out of the way, but then Kove hesitated and finally dropped his balled fist. It took Ryon a moment to make a decision, but in the end, he moved off Kove.

"You broke my fucking nose," Kove growled as he pulled himself up to sit, readjusting his nose.

"You broke my fucking ribs," Ryon gritted out through the pain as his eyes darted to Laina. She still stood against the far wall, her hand up against her mouth and looking as though she wasn't sure whether to interfere or stay where she was. He was glad she decided on the latter.

"You brought this on yourself," Kove sneered, dragging Ryon's attention back to him. "If you had wiped her memory like you should have, I wouldn't be here right now."

"She won't tell anyone," he hissed in response. "And do you think that it even matters after what happened last night? We'll be front-page news by the morning!"

Kove pushed himself back against the lounge and used his hand to wipe away the blood at his nose. "Those humans had their minds wiped."

"That you know of. What if someone was missed, Kove?" Ryon retorted.

Kove shook his head, lifting his knees up to rest his elbows on them. He turned to Ryon, the blood now dried on his face. "No one was missed. And besides, even if—on the off chance —someone did make it out with their memory intact, no one would believe them. But *this*," he gestured to Laina. "This is different. You didn't forget to wipe her memory, you *let* her go. Why?"

Why indeed, Ryon thought. How to answer that...*because I selfishly want her to remember me? Because I have a ridiculous urge to protect this little human and her mind? Because I want her?*

Kove sighed and pulled himself up to stand when Ryon didn't respond. "Do the right thing," Kove said, glancing over at Laina, then back to Ryon. "Don't lose my trust just because you think you've got *hers*." And then he was gone.

CHAPTER FOURTEEN

L aina watched as the male—*Kove*—straightened his leather jacket and then disappeared. He just upped and *vanished*. Her eyes riveted to the place in her living room where Kove had been standing only moments ago.

"It's called fading," Ryon said, his eyes flickering with gold. *Was it emotion that caused them to flicker and glow?*

He ran a hand through his dishevelled hair. Her eyes caught the movement, and she found herself wondering how that hair would feel against her own fingertips.

When Ryon continued to speak, she tore her gaze from his hair and met those mesmerising eyes once more. "As long as there's a window or a door open, we can fade in or out of wherever we are, straight to wherever we have to go."

Huh. "Without an invitation?" she asked.

Ryon chuckled and then winced before he reached back and unsheathed a sword from his back. Placing it on the floor beside him, he shuffled over to lean back against the lounge. "The whole invitation thing is a myth. Vampires don't need to be invited in." He pulled up his knees and rested his elbows on them. "Are you okay?"

She nodded, and that was when the adrenaline left her body. No longer able to stand upright, she slowly sunk down the wall until she was seated on the floor, her position mirroring Ryon's.

After a moment, she said, "thank you...for coming. For helping." He gave a reluctant nod as the silence stretched out between them. Then something dawned on her. "H-how did you know where I lived? How did *he* know?" She wanted to ask if Ryon really had been outside her kitchen window last night but that kind of felt irrelevant now.

"We have a friend who's exceptionally good at finding people," he said matter-of-factly.

"That man that was here..." her voice trailed off, and she swallowed down the knot that had formed in her throat.

"Male," he corrected. "Male. Boy vampires are called males. Humans are called men. And the same goes for the girls —females for vampires. Women for humans."

"Oh." Laina found her gaze dropping to the pink, blue, and white stripes of her pyjama pants. There was a whole world out there that she had no idea about. She used to think Ladwick was small, tiny even. Everyone knew each other and no one could go on a date without the entire town knowing. But now she realised, she was just a tiny fish in a much bigger ocean and there was a whole ecosystem out there that she never knew existed.

"He wouldn't have hurt you." Ryon's voice pulled her out of her thoughts, and she glanced up to see him rest his head back against the chair, looking up at the ceiling. "He would have wiped your memory, but he wouldn't have hurt you."

"Why?" Laina asked softly. When Ryon's head turned in her direction, there was no longer gold flickering in those brown eyes. And suddenly he looked so...so *human*. "Why did you stop him from wiping my mind?"

"I don't know," he said honestly. "I've never broken the rules before."

Laina frowned at that. "Rules?"

Ryon lay his head back again. He looked pensively at the ceiling, as if it could give him the advice he was searching for. After a moment, he said, "I belong to a...a group of vampire enforcers. We ensure all vampires in Ladwick abide by the rules to never kill a human and wipe their memories after a feeding."

Laina's stomach churned with the information. "H-how many vampires are there in Ladwick?"

He shrugged. "After sundown they're everywhere. Bar tending in clubs, waiting in restaurants, Uber drivers, you name it. They live their lives just like humans do, only at night." He glanced at her. "But they're in control of their blood lust. The vampires in that alley the other night and in the hospital, the one that tried to..." he shook his head. "There are vampires out there that can't control their need for blood, and they're the ones that are killing humans."

Laina could only blink as Ryon's words sunk in. Vampires were...*everywhere?* And the vampires that couldn't control their blood lust...had one of them killed her parents? She pushed away those thoughts as her mind began to form questions.

"Have...have you ever killed a human?"

Ryon's brows drew together, and he looked over at her. "Never."

Laina's relief was short lived when his words from earlier sunk in. *Feeding. From blood.* "How often do you f-feed?"

"Every night. We can eat food too, but blood is the only thing that sustains us." *Every night?* "But I don't take blood without giving in return," he added.

She frowned. Was he trying to *justify* it? "What do you mean?" she asked, suddenly aware that she was now having a casual conversation with a...*Vampire.*

He shrugged, the tension in his shoulders making him look anything but casual. "The women don't leave empty handed, if you know what I mean." After a moment he said, "a bit of give and take."

Laina's eyes widened as she realised what he meant. *Women. Give and take.* "So, you drink women's blood in exchange for *sex*?"

"Not sex...not exactly," he replied. Laina didn't miss the way he shuffled awkwardly where he sat.

"Do you drink from men too?" she asked abruptly, unsure why she even cared.

He shook his head. "I don't, but plenty of vampires do." He shrugged once more. "Just a preference."

Laina nodded, her head feeling like it would explode from the onslaught of information. Then she asked, "how old are you?"

"Old," he answered with a snort, sending her a quick glance before returning his attention to the bar.

"Are you immortal?"

"No. Despite what the myths say, vampires are not immortal. We just live a very long time and age *very* slowly, but we're not immortal."

Laina bit the inside of her cheek as she considered what he'd said. "Are you...dead?"

He smirked. "Not where it counts."

That smirk. That innuendo. The way his eyes lifted. The way his lips curled up and the way she could see a hint of his sharp, white fangs. The combination should scare her, but instead it sent butterflies exploding into a million tiny little flutters that reverberated through her entire body.

"Technically," he continued, "we are dead, yes. Our hearts don't need to beat, and our lungs don't need to breathe, but thanks to muscle memory from our lives as humans, our bodies still work the same."

"So, you were a human once?" She watched with curiosity as he glanced away from her and looked down at his arm—no, his hand. He turned it over in his lap and that was when she saw it. The *scars*. It looked as though he'd been burned, and badly. And it made Max's own hand look like it truly *did* only need a band aid in comparison.

"Yes. But we don't remember our lives as humans," he said cryptically. "Anyway," he pushed himself to stand, wincing slightly as he picked up his sword and sheathed it again. "I don't know why I told you that. I guess after what you've witnessed, it doesn't really matter anymore."

Laina stayed where she was. A ripple of apprehension ran through her as she asked, "are you going to wipe my memory now?" After letting her go in the alley and again last night without wiping her memory, she wasn't sure if he would change his mind and do it now. But either way, she wanted to know.

"That depends," he said, turning to her, those brown eyes meeting her own. "Are you going to tell anyone?"

She shook her head. "No."

He searched her face, his gaze roaming over her as if he were looking for a sign that she was lying. After a moment he gave a curt nod. "Then no, I won't take away your memory." Did he look...relieved?

Ryon turned and headed for the patio door, but something inside of Laina screamed out to tell him to stay. She pushed herself up to stand just as he reached the open door. She heard herself say, "I lost both my parents six months ago."

He froze. His broad shoulders tensed in that leather jacket of his before he slowly turned around to face her, his expression a mix of curiosity and sympathy. She swallowed hard and walked over to the lounge, sinking into it. She had no idea what she was doing, opening up like this, but it just felt...*right* to be telling him. He'd given her a little piece of his world, and now she wanted to give a little piece of herself in return.

She glanced down and trailed the stripes on her pyjama pants. "They were...they were going out for dinner. My sister and I were meant to go with them, but we both pulled out. Brynn had just broken up with her boyfriend—none of us had met him and they'd only been going out a few months, but she was pretty shaken by the breakup and wanted to stay in for the night instead. I was out with Max and a few of our friends at the time."

She didn't look up, but she heard Ryon's footsteps before he sat down in the seat beside her, close enough that their knees touched. Her eyes darted to where his strong and powerful jean-clad legs came up against her thin pyjamas. Despite the fabric between them, she could feel the warmth of his body, proving that the theory that vampires had cold skin was yet another myth.

Ryon remained quiet, and she realised he was giving her the space and time to keep going. "Sometimes..." her voice cracked, so she tried again. "Sometimes, I wonder if..." a sob left her as tears began to well in her eyes. "I wonder if things would be different today if I had been with them. If Brynn had been with them." She inhaled deeply and wiped away the tears, straightening on the lounge. She just wanted to give Ryon a small piece of her, not fall apart in front of him.

"How did they die?" he asked softly.

Laina leaned forward, resting her elbows on her knees, and scrubbing her hands over her face. It took her a moment to compose herself enough to say the word. After all, this was the first time she was admitting it out loud. "Vampires."

She heard Ryon let out a curse before he shuffled beside her, his leather jacket creaking with the movement. "I...I don't know what to say Laina. I'm so sorry." After a moment he added, "if there was a way that I could find who did it; If I could track them down, I would destroy them for what they did to your parents. To you."

Laina's breath hitched at the honesty in his words. He'd meant it. And with the way he took care of the vampire in front of her last night at the hospital, she knew he'd follow through on that promise too. Composing herself, she leaned back on the lounge again and glanced over at him. "You're not what I expected for a vampire," she observed.

The edges of his lips curled into a smirk again. "You're not what I expected for a human."

To her surprise and despite everything that had happened, Laina felt the edges of her own lips begin to curl. "Why not?"

He seemed to relax at her playful tone. He sunk further into the lounge and laid an arm along the back of it, his hand almost touching the back of her neck. "For starters, you're not afraid to ask questions."

His smile widened as she chuckled and even though she could clearly see his fangs, she still felt safe. She knew now, without a shadow of a doubt, that he wouldn't hurt her.

"And after the last two nights, you haven't checked yourself into the nearest psychiatric unit, so there's that," he said.

Laina laughed—actually *laughed*. And *God,* did it feel good to laugh. It was so absurd to even be laughing after the things she'd witnessed but...he was right. After everything that had happened, she was lucky not to be in a padded cell, curled up in a corner and rocking back and forth.

"And you're beautiful," he said, his voice low and husky.

Laina's heart somersaulted in her chest as the laughter died in her throat. When Max had called her beautiful, her stomach had twisted with dread at his words. But hearing Ryon say it? And in that tone of voice? It seemed to trigger something inside of her body that sent ripples of excitement to every nerve ending.

She glanced over and met his light brown eyes. As if he'd only just realised what he'd said, he closed his eyes and gave a shake of his head. "I should go," he said, standing abruptly.

Laina stood, heart thumping wildly in her chest as she threw all logic aside to ask, "why did you really stop that man —*male*," she corrected, "from wiping my memory?" She may have been completely wrong in her assumption, but suddenly she didn't think Ryon stopped that male from wiping her memory *only* because she'd asked him not to.

Ryon turned around and stepped closer to her. He reached forward, hesitating before running his fingers over her cheekbone and down to her chin.

Surprising herself, she didn't pull back. She didn't even flinch.

His face grew serious, and as if her lack of reaction gave him the permission he was looking for, he cupped her cheek. "Because there's something about you that feels important to me," he said. "And call me selfish...but I want you to remember me."

"I...I want to remember you too," she said, honestly. And it was true. She didn't just want to remember the fact that vampires existed, she wanted to remember Ryon. To remember what he'd done for her and how he made her feel. When she was around him, she felt safe, she felt special and right now, under his heated gaze, she felt like his *world*.

It was in that moment that Laina realised that there was a connection between them she could no longer deny. She swallowed hard as excitement and anticipation warred within her. She wanted this. She wanted *him*...but a part of her—a niggling voice deep down, whispered that this was wrong. That he was a vampire. But he was different from the rest, and she knew it in her soul. She'd watched his strong arms thrust a sword into another vampire's skull, and she'd watched him pull back a clenched fist only to thrust it forward and break Kove's nose. He'd been so fierce, so violent, yet he had shown her he was capable of being gentle—Not only gentle, that he was capable of being kind, charming, funny, handsome, and *sexy*.

Ryon's gaze turned heavy-lidded and Laina's tongue darted out to moisten her bottom lip. Ryon didn't miss the movement. His eyes flared with gold, proving her theory about that eye colour changing with emotion, as they dipped to her lips. The intensity in his gaze was undeniable as the chemistry between them continued to build. He stepped closer and that connection between them became tangible, palpable and...*desperate.* And Laina couldn't take anymore.

And clearly, neither could Ryon.

"I need to kiss you." Ryon's deep voice was like a trigger, igniting an explosion of arousal that rippled through her body and ended in a quivering heat between her legs.

"Kiss me," she breathed. Was that even her voice? It was so sultry, so *breathy*, she didn't even recognise herself.

Ryon leaned forward as Laina's breaths grew shallow, her heart thumping wildly in her chest. And then his lips were on hers. Hard. Hot. Desperate. She closed her eyes when she felt Ryon's hands on her. On her sides, on her arms and running up and down her body until they rested on her hips, giving them a small squeeze. Her hands reached out to his warm chest. She could feel the hard panes of his pecs through his thin t-shirt, and it made her want to take it off him so she could see more, *feel* more of him.

She moaned into his closed mouth when he pressed his body against hers and she felt that other parts of him were just as hard. *God,* she wanted him. *Needed* him. One of his hands released her hip to come up and cradle the back of her head as he took advantage of her open mouth. He tilted his head, deepening the kiss and letting out a moan of his own as their tongues touched for the first time. And then she was lost. Ryon set a rhythm, their tongues entwining in a sensual dance of wet heat as she ran her hands up to his shoulders and pushed at his leather jacket. He released her with a smirk that said he knew exactly what she wanted.

He pulled back and attempted to shrug out of his jacket— only to grunt in pain.

"You're hurt!" she said with a gasp.

He shook his head and slowly—*painfully*—shucked the leather jacket, throwing it off to the side with the sword still sheathed. "I'm not *that* hurt. Besides, I'll heal soon. I just need to sit down."

She knew she was gaping at him as he sat on the lounge, sinking into it. "Heal?"

He leaned forward and smiled, that smile enough to melt her clothes right off her. "That's right, we can heal too."

She saw him fight back a wince as he reached out to her, wrapping his big hands around the back of her thighs and pulling her closer. Her breaths quickened as she let him guide her until she stood between his legs. His hands roamed up her legs to her backside, giving each cheek a gentle squeeze as he looked up at her, his expression turning serious. "You're so *fucking* beautiful." She let out a mewl and threw her head back as his hands found their way to the inside of her thighs and began moving upwards in a slow, tantalising ascent.

Her hands found his hair, and she finally let herself run her hands through it, gripping it and eliciting a moan from him as his fingers traced over her core. Even through her thin pyjama pants, she could feel the heat from his touch against her most sensitive parts.

She looked down at him as his hands moved to her legs, and he guided her to climb into his lap, straddling him. Was she really doing this? *Yes, yes, I am*, she thought as she ran her hands through his hair again.

Ryon palmed her backside once more before one hand made its way up to cup her head and pull her back down to his lips. And what a kisser he was. He *devoured* her. She was so lost in the kiss, their tongues moving with and against each other, that she didn't notice his hands as they pulled down her tank top. She gasped against his mouth when he cupped her breast, and he didn't waste time, pulling back and covering her other breast with his mouth.

"Oh, God," she whispered, throwing her head back as she ground into him—right over his rock-hard erection.

"*Fuck,*" he growled against her breast before she did it again, rubbing herself over his length and relishing in the feel of it between her legs. He let out a moan as he moved to her other breast and thrust his hips up to meet hers, their bodies grinding together and sending them both into a tailspin of building pleasure.

More. Laina needed more. She let go of his hair and reached for the waistband of his jeans. He threw his head back, his mouth parting and showing those sharp fangs as he closed his eyes, savouring in the ecstasy of the moment. She didn't bother to unbuckle, unbutton, or unzip as she squeezed her fingers inside the waistband, brushing her fingertips against the slick head of his erection. No underwear. He was wearing no underwear. He opened his eyes and hissed at the contact before she pulled her hand away, groaning at the thought of how easily and quickly she could expose his length. At how easily and quickly he could be inside of her.

"Fuck, I want you," he said, his voice straining. His eyes turned from brown to gold as they roamed over Laina's face, neck, and exposed breasts. She should feel vulnerable under his gaze, but his expression was one of awe, of reverence, and any sliver of self-consciousness she felt withered away.

"I want you too," she breathed out as those eyes met hers once more.

Ryon took her face in his hands and pulled her down for

another desperate kiss as their bodies continued to move together, stroking each other. When they were both wanton, panting and on the verge of a release, Ryon pulled back from the kiss and moved down. He kissed, licked, and sucked, leaving a trail of burning heat as he made his way from her mouth to her cheek, her chin...then her neck.

And then everything happened so fast that it took Laina's brain a moment to catch up.

One second, she was experiencing the most intensely erotic moment of her life, and the next, there was blood.

Laina felt a sharp sting at her neck before Ryon pulled back abruptly, his golden eyes wide with shock. She recoiled on a gasp, her eyes riveted to the crimson liquid on his lips. His tongue darted out to taste the blood, and his eyes flared a brighter gold—if that were even possible. Laina's hand lifted to her neck, her fingers finding slippery warmth where she'd felt that sting. *Blood.* She was bleeding. And when she pulled back her hand and glanced at her fingertips, it confirmed her suspicions. Ryon had...*bitten* her.

She lifted her tank top to cover her breasts as she scrambled back, away from Ryon where he continued to sit, wide-eyed, tense, and frozen on the lounge. "I..." he started, his hand lifting to wipe the blood from his lips—*her* blood. "I...I didn't mean to. It...it was an accident," he whispered, pushing himself up to stand.

"You bit me," she said, in shock as she took another step back. She *shouldn't* have been shocked, though. Should she? After all, Ryon was a vampire, and she had been a fool to think he was any different to those vampires in the alley or the hospital. He'd even admitted that he fed on human blood every night. *A bit of give and take.* His words returned to her in a

96

rush as she began to piece it all together. "This is what you do," she finally looked up at him. "Isn't it?" It was as if a bucket of freezing cold water had been poured over her head, and she was thrown back into reality. He was a vampire, and she was a human. The breath caught in her throat as she realised everything that he had said to her had been a lie. She wasn't important to him—she was *food*.

He frowned, taking a step forward. Shaking his head, he started to ask, "what do you—"

But she cut him off by throwing his own words back at him. "A bit of give and take."

"What? No. Laina." He stepped forward again, but she only stepped back, wrapping her hands around herself. He looked genuinely remorseful...but how did she know that wasn't part of his ploy? How did she know this entire thing wasn't just an act, and he was playing with his food?

"Get out," she said softly, her gaze dropping to the ground as shame threatened her knees to give out. She'd almost given herself up to a vampire. To the enemy. To someone of the same kind that had killed her parents. "Get *out*!" she yelled as anger overwhelmed her. Anger that she knew was not just aimed at him but also at herself.

CHAPTER FIFTEEN

When Ryon materialised on the front lawn of the manor, his chest was aching with a pain that had nothing to do with his healing ribs. He'd fucked up. In the heat of the moment, he'd pierced the pale skin at her neck with his fangs. He hadn't meant to, but the need to have her in every way was nigh impossible to deny. His fangs had barely pushed through the surface when he realised what he had done and pulled back, shocked at his actions. And Laina... those green eyes of hers had looked at him as if he'd betrayed her. And he had. She'd trusted him and he'd ruined it. The anger in her eyes when she'd yelled at him to leave was something he'd never forget. It had taken a minute for him to accept defeat and fade out of her apartment.

But he needed to see her again. He needed to go to her and try to make things right even though he had no idea *how*. *Fuck.* He ran a hand through his hair and began to pace around the grounds. He wasn't ready to go inside. He wasn't ready to face Kove and the others when his stomach was twisting in knots like this, making him want to retch.

The sound of a notification echoed from Ryon's back pocket, and he stopped pacing to pull out his phone. A text from Soran.

Meeting in my office in 5.

Ryon sighed and placed the phone back in his pocket. He still wasn't ready to head inside, but he could use the distraction.

A few minutes later, Ryon made his way inside the manor and up the stairs. And as it turned out, the text from Soran hadn't just been for him—all the Shadows stood outside the office. Before he reached them, the office door swung open to show a still red-eyed Zane standing just inside. "Come in."

The Shadow members cast a curious glance at each other before they began to pile inside. *What was Zane doing in Soran's office?* Ryon watched as the Shadows all made their way into the room before him, all except for Kove. Kove stood in the doorway, his knowing eyes locked on Ryon for a moment.

"You reek of human," Kove said, then he turned and joined the others in the room before Ryon could respond.

Ryon was the last to enter the office, gritting his teeth as he did so. He tore his gaze from where he'd been glaring at Kove to see that...Soran wasn't anywhere to be seen.

"Welcome, gentle males."

Ryon's gaze darted over to the male figure by the window. He wore a gold crown with thorns around the base, his long dark hair pulled back in a ponytail underneath, and a black shirt tucked neatly into black trousers. The power emanating from the male filled the room—and if anyone doubted who he was, the emblem on the front of his shirt confirmed it. *King Cazimir Drosera.* The red embroidered crest with the initials C and D overlapping sat stark against the black material behind it. It matched the pattern of the rug that spanned the hallway and every room in the manor.

King Drosera's eyes glowed pure gold as they raked over each Shadow member but then stopped on Ryon. Like the paintings out in the hallway, the King had masculine features, with thick, dark eyebrows, a strong jaw, and a straight nose. But the paintings in the hall did nothing to show the intensity in the King's gaze—something that Ryon suddenly felt he'd seen somewhere before. The air in the room grew thick with tension as King Drosera tore his gaze from Ryon and walked over to Soran's chair before casually sinking into it.

"I don't believe introductions are necessary. I'm sure by now you all know who I am," the King said. Zane took that moment to close the door and move to stand behind the King's—no, Soran's—chair.

"Where's Soran?" someone asked.

"Soran won't be coming back." A chorus of '*how*,' '*what*,' and '*why*' rang out, but Ryon stayed silent, deep dread creeping into his stomach. King Drosera stood and slammed his hand down on the desk, cracking the wood and forcing everyone into silence again. He adjusted his crown and took a moment to compose himself before he sat down again. "Unfortunately, Soran's values no longer align with those of the sovereignty." Rage exploded in Ryon, and he took a step forward to say something, but Fynn pulled him back with a firm hand on his arm.

King Drosera's gaze snapped to Ryon and held there before glancing around at everyone. "I understand that this news has come as somewhat of a shock, but times are changing, and we need to move forward." The King stood and looked every bit the regal monarch as he moved around the office with his hands behind his back. "For too long, vampires have abided by the rules. We have lived in the shadows, forced to stay hidden away from humans. But no longer."

Ryon glanced over to see the rest of the Shadow members looking between themselves, their expressions a mix of curiosity and confusion. Everyone but Kove that was. His gaze was locked on the King, his own expression vacant.

"I came here tonight to personally advise you I will be disbanding the Shadows as of midnight tonight." *What?* The dread inside of Ryon exploded into disbelief, and the silence in the room told Ryon that the others were just as shocked as he was. "The need for enforcers will be redundant as there will no longer be rules to abide."

"Without rules," Kove spoke up, his face still expressionless. "Humans will know about us within a week."

"Precisely," the King said, flashing his long fangs as he smiled. "And when they do," the King said through a sneer. "You kill them. You show them what we're capable of." *Kill them?* Ryon was speechless—as were the other Shadows. The King paused, but only for a moment. "My dear gentle males, you have played by the rules here as Shadows members for too long." The King placed a hand over his deadened heart. "Whilst I am grateful for your service to the crown as enforcers, I have deliberated over this for a long time. And that time is *now*. It is time to show the world who is at the top of the food chain."

"Us!" The King bellowed, his features suddenly pulled tight in anger. "*We* are at the top of the food chain! It is the humans who should be afraid of us!" He inhaled and ran a hand down the front of his shirt, straightening it.

"Why now?" Ryon demanded. King Drosera appeared in

front of him in the blink of an eye, fading so fast that Ryon barely caught himself from stepping back with surprise.

"Are you questioning me, *boy*?"

Boy. That word. Ryon had been called that before...but where? Pushing those thoughts away, he met the King's stare brazenly. "I want to know what's changed."

"What's *changed*?" the King sneered. "Why does anything have to *change* for history to be righted?" They stared at each other, unflinching, until the King turned away.

"Now," the King began in a calmer tone as he moved back to sit on the corner of the desk. "As I'm sure you are all aware, my reign covers all the Garabitha Region, but I have chosen Ladwick to begin our ascension to power. And what happens in Ladwick will be an example of what will occur in each town. If you choose to join me in taking back what is ours, you may continue to reside here in this manor. However, you will need to join me in the palace *this* evening to discuss our plans for the future. Should you wish to stay there, you are most welcome. I assure you, there are plenty of rooms in the palace for you all. There are servants, food, alcohol," he paused with a smile that looked anything but genuine. "Females, or males, whichever you'd prefer. I can assure you all your needs will be met."

"And if we don't?" Fynn asked. The King tilted his head, his smile widening—and then he was gone.

Fynn jumped as King Drosera suddenly appeared behind him. "Would you like to find out?" he whispered.

"No, I'm good," Fynn rushed out, raising his hands placatingly. After a moment, the King nodded and strode for the front of the room.

"What about the humans?" Ryon asked, his thoughts

immediately going to Laina as a sinking feeling crept into his gut.

"No longer our problem," Xavier said, stepping forward to stand beside the King as Malik and Rune followed suit.

"I'm in," Damien said, stepping forward with Darick.

Only Kove, Fynn, and Ryon remained, and Ryon's chest tightened as he looked over at them. He wanted to protect Laina from all this. He *needed* to. But could he do that while protecting the very thing that wanted her dead? He couldn't turn his back on his people, on his King...could he?

And then what about Soran? Soran had been something like a father to him. What had happened to him? Had King Drosera killed him? A wave of grief rocked him on his heels at the thought. And if Ryon refused to work with the King, would his fate be the same? And what of Laina then?

King Drosera began to talk to those around him as Kove stepped forward. Ryon didn't hesitate. He gripped Kove's arm so tightly that his former friend turned back to him with a snarl.

Ryon shook his head and whispered, "this doesn't feel right, Kove, and you know it."

Kove narrowed his eyes. "Tell me something," he said in a low voice. "That human woman tonight. Did you wipe her memory?"

Ryon tensed, and he knew Kove had hit him where it hurt. His lips thinned as he dropped Kove's arm.

"Didn't think so," Kove said, his tone filled with disappointment. "Way I see it. We're fucked as a species either way. And I'd rather be on the winning team."

Ryon watched as Kove joined the others, and Fynn came

up beside him. "Kove's right. There's not much of a choice here. Best not to fight a losing battle."

Ryon's stomach sunk to the floor as Fynn walked over to the group, leaving him alone. King Drosera looked over at him, his eyes boring into Ryon's own with a questioning glance—a *challenging* glance. With clenched teeth and a heavy heart, Ryon put one foot in front of the other and joined them. If not to ensure his own safety, then to ensure Laina's.

Fynn was wrong when he said there was not much of a choice.

There was no choice at all.

CHAPTER SIXTEEN

You need the money, Laina told herself as she drove to her new client's house. She generally dealt with clients over email, but the older woman had called and explained that she had no internet and no email address, so Laina was on the way to a face-to-face meeting. Going by what the woman had said over the phone, it would be a quick job as she only needed a logo for a new Quilting business she'd just started. Honestly, it probably cost more in petrol to get out here than she'd make on the job...but then again, as her dad used to say, '*a job's a job*'.

Laina took the exit ramp that would take her an extra twenty minutes in the opposite direction before rounding back to Dultri Heights. Just so she could bypass Oak Hills. She didn't need to go anywhere near where her parents were killed.

In fact, this was the first time she'd been in the vicinity of Oak Hills since it happened. And despite her attempts to stay focused on the driving, her mind was a mess. Images of her parents, the vampires in the alleyway, the hospital, and Ryon last night all circled her mind, making it hard to concentrate.

He bit me, she thought as she recalled Ryon pulling back from her neck, her blood staining his lips. Her heart felt like lead as she gritted her teeth and slammed her hand down on the steering wheel. *Dammit*, she'd trusted him. She thought he was different. He may not have killed her, but he could have—and he'd proven that last night. She had no idea what made him pull back instead of continuing to drink her blood, but that was irrelevant, wasn't it? The fact of the matter remained. She'd trusted him not to hurt her—and he did.

Before she knew it, Laina had reached Dultri Heights and was pulling up to a quaint little cottage with a white picket fence and rose bushes scattered in the front yard. She let out a sigh and mentally prepared herself to plaster on a smile and a cheerful disposition. *You need the money*, she repeated to herself.

Laina collected her phone and notebook and placed them in her handbag before making her way to the front door to knock. It wasn't even five seconds before an elderly woman came to the door as if she'd been standing just inside it the entire time. She was short and curvy and wore a blue floral blouse, black slacks, and fluffy pink slippers. She pushed her glasses up her nose, and Laina noticed that there were still grey strands throughout her short, white bob of hair.

"Hi!" Laina said with a smile that she hoped looked more genuine than it felt. "My name is Laina from L.H. Designs, and you must be Mrs Conner?"

"Oh, yes! Do come in! And please, call me Wendy." She opened the door wider and gestured inside.

Laina gave a polite smile and stepped into the cottage. "Nice to meet you, Wendy," she said as she followed the older woman down the hallway.

Coming into the dining area, Laina took in the various knick-knacks and family photos scattered around the room on shelves before sitting down at the dining table opposite Wendy.

"Nice to meet you too, my dear. And thank you for coming out to see me. I'm not very handy with a computer, you see," Wendy said with a soft chuckle. She pointed to the teacup and mugs already set out on the table, "would you like a cup of tea or coffee before we begin?"

"Actually, a cup of tea sounds wonderful, thank you." Laina went about making her tea as Wendy got up from the table and disappeared into the kitchen, only to come back with a tray of cookies.

"I bake these every week," she said, placing the cookies on the table. "They were my grandson's favourite. He seemed to have a knack for knowing when I'd bake them, and as soon as they were out of the oven, he'd be a-knocking on the door. My husband—God rest his soul—used to say that Fredrick would come just for the cookies, but I know, he loved our company too." *Loved?*

Laina picked up a cookie. "Oh, has he moved away?"

Wendy's eyes glistened, and she shook her head. "No, he passed. Or at least we believe he has passed. His...he was never found."

He was never found? Laina lifted a hand to her mouth, mortified. "Oh, my goodness, I'm so sorry. I shouldn't have—"

Wendy cut her off, waving a hand dismissively. "Oh no, my dear. I'm the one who's sorry. You came here to discuss designs, not to hear me harp on about my life."

Laina fought the urge to go over and throw her arms

around the older woman. So far, the only thing Laina knew about her was that she'd lost her husband *and* her grandson. And somewhere along the lines, she'd decided to start up her own quilting business. Wendy was trying to move on. She was trying to pick her life up after suffering through such incomprehensible loss. Laina knew all too well what that felt like.

"Will you tell me about him?" Laina found herself asking. "What was he like?"

Wendy's eyes widened before a smile spread over her lips. Beaming, she replied, "Oh, he was such a wonderful, cheeky boy who grew up to be an even better man." She let out a chuckle. "He was so funny. He used to find a way to make everything light-hearted." She grew silent and began to smooth a wrinkle out of the floral tablecloth. "His parents had him when they were very young. His father decided he wasn't ready for a child and disappeared, and his mother...well, let's just say my daughter spiralled after that and fell in with the wrong crowd. She passed when Fredrick was just six, and we took over caring for him after that." Her eyes darted up to Laina, whose chest clenched at the story. Wendy had experienced more loss than Laina could even imagine. "We would worry that Fredrick himself would spiral without his mother and father around, but he proved us wrong. He did have one bad habit, though—he smoked. We used to try to get him to stop, but he never did. He was engaged, you know?"

"Oh?" Wendy abruptly stood and went over to one of the bookshelves and picked up a picture frame. Coming back to the table, Wendy held out the frame, and Laina felt her eyes blur with tears for the young couple in the photo. The man was handsome with spiky light brown hair, a groomed goatee, and bright blue eyes. He looked like a Hemsworth brother in his late twenties, and the woman he had his arm around looked like she'd just strolled off the catwalk. She was thin with long blonde hair curled into ringlets at the base and bright blue eyes. The happy couple were dressed nicely—the woman wore a figure-hugging blue strapless dress, and the man wore a crisp blue shirt and black trousers.

"This was taken at their engagement party a few weeks before...before it happened," Wendy said sadly. "Fredrick was walking Elizabeth home from the cinema—they loved the cinema—and that was when they were attacked. Elizabeth was found with..." Wendy lifted her hand to her throat but then lowered it. "Elizabeth's body was found, but Fredrick's never was. That was ten years ago this summer."

Laina wanted to say something. She wanted to pass on her condolences, but her eyes remained fixated on the couple in the photo. What happened to them? When Wendy's hand went to her throat, Laina thought maybe they suffered the same fate as her parents. But then again, Wendy said this happened ten years ago, and things like that weren't happening that long ago, were they?

"Oh dear," Wendy said on a sigh, snapping Laina out of her thoughts. Wendy pulled back the frame, stood from the table and made her way over to the shelves to put it back. "I get so carried away talking about Fredrick sometimes. Anyway, my dear, I'm sure your time is valuable, so let's get back to business."

"That's no problem at all. And again, I'm sorry for your loss," Laina said, unsure what else to say. For the second time in half an hour, she fought back the urge to give the woman a big hug.

"Have you ever lost anyone, my dear?" Wendy asked,

sitting back down at the table. The question threw Laina, but the kind eyes staring across at her made her feel comfortable enough to open up.

"Yes, actually, my parents."

Wendy gasped and covered her mouth with her hand. "Oh my, that must have been so hard for you, dear." Laina swallowed hard but managed a small smile as Wendy reached across the table to take her hand. "When we hold on to the memories of those we loved, there is no true loss. They are with us always—in here," Wendy patted her chest with her free hand. "And I have no doubt that your parents would be so proud of you."

Laina's vision blurred with tears. Truth be told, she wasn't sure her parents would be proud of her at all. *God*, she was falling apart in a stranger's house. Wendy handed her a tissue that she accepted with a smile and wiped her eyes. "Thank you," Laina said, inhaling to compose herself. "So, you were telling me over the phone that you are starting your own quilting business?"

Wendy's face lit up, and she sat back. "Yes! I have dabbled in quilt making, and a few of the ladies in the seniors' club have told me they are good enough to sell, but I need a business card and a...what do you call it? A symbol? No, an icon?"

"A logo?"

"Yes! A logo!" Wendy said, clapping her hands together excitedly. Laina couldn't help but let out a chuckle at that. "Anyway, Barbara, at the seniors' club, told me about how her daughter used your services to make a brand name and icon— I'm sorry, a *logo*—for her new clothing store. So, she passed on your details, and here you are!"

"Ah, Rainbow Threads? Denise?" Laina asked, thinking

back to when she'd first started freelancing. Denise had been one of her first clients.

"That's the one!" Wendy said before explaining what she wanted the brand name and logo to look like. Laina pulled out her notebook and began to take notes—and as predicted, this would be a quick and easy job. And for some reason, a sinking feeling started in the pit of her stomach at the thought. Wendy emanated pure maternal warmth, and it wasn't until now that Laina realised why she'd be sad to leave this place. It was because Wendy reminded her of her mother.

CHAPTER SEVENTEEN

Ryon awoke to his mothers' scream. He rushed out of bed and opened the door to his bedroom, knowing what he was about to see. He'd been here before. He'd seen this before. But as much as he knew what was about to happen, he couldn't do anything about it. He watched in terror as his mother was dragged, kicking, and screaming down the hallway and then to the living room. He ran to the man who seemed to be in charge and started begging for them to release his mother. Words were spoken, but unlike the last time Ryon had this dream, he wasn't listening.

Instead, he focused on the crest at the shoulder of the red robe before him. It looked familiar.

The sound of his mother's scream had him tearing his gaze away from the robe and twisting around to see his mother thrown out into the daylight sun. He sprinted to the door and reached out a hand into the burning sun as his mother cried out. *You're better than him!* The guards pulled him back inside as his mother disintegrated into a fine dusting of black ash. He knew what would come next. The pain. The twin burns of agony in his hand and his chest, both blazing with flames of intense anguish that made him want to retch.

The streaming rays of sunlight dimmed as Ryon glanced up to see that someone had closed the door, and he could no longer see the place where his mother last stood. A figure stepped in front of him, and Ryon watched the red velvet robe of the male as he squatted down until they were face-to-face. But before Ryon could see the face of the male who killed his mother, he squeezed his eyes shut. He was next. They killed his mother, and now they'd kill him.

———

Ryon sprung up in bed, covered in sweat and panting. *It is only a dream. Only a dream—the* same *dream as last night. But still, only a dream.* But when he glanced around the unfamiliar room, he wondered if it had been a dream after all. The room style was ornate, with gold and white patterned wallpaper covering every wall. There was a dark mahogany wardrobe, a door that seemed to lead to a marble bathroom and a double panelled window with the shutters drawn closed. This wasn't his room. And it took Ryon a full minute to recall where he was. The palace.

After following the King and fading to the palace last night, the head butler had shown them to their rooms and then down to the dining hall so they could share a meal together. Food wasn't necessary for vampires, but they could eat if they wanted to. And with all the extravagant food that had been brought to the table? They wanted to. Then had come the warm blood served in detailed golden chalices.

Unlike the blood bags they kept chilled in the manor, this tasted *fresh*.

By the time they had finished their meals, their belongings had been brought over, the numerous maids and butlers having collected them from the manor. Ryon had showered in the adjoining bathroom and then tried to get some shut eye. He'd tossed and turned, his mind running through everything that had happened with Laina, Kove, Soran, the King and his new plan. None of it had sat well with him. He'd been a vampire now for a hundred years. Like all the other vampires in Ladwick, he'd always had confidence that the King had their best interests at heart...but he wasn't so sure anymore. And what had happened to Soran? He needed him. They all did...but he had a sinking feeling he'd never see Soran again.

Ryon pushed away the thought and considered what the King had planned. Or what he could possibly have planned that wouldn't put the species at risk. Ryon couldn't understand how forgoing all the rules and exposing themselves to humans at night would serve as anything more than putting a target on their backs during the day. Last night, after what felt like hours, sleep had finally consumed him...only for him to wake from that strange dream again.

Scrubbing a hand over his face, Ryon rolled over and looked at the time on his phone. Midday. The sun was at the highest point of the day and would only begin its descent in another five or so hours. He'd have to wait until then to find Laina and try to make amends. He didn't know how she'd feel seeing him again, but he had to see her and, at the very least, warn her about the King's plan.

He threw off the covers with a sigh and pulled on some grey slacks and a black t-shirt. He didn't think the King would appreciate Ryon exploring the palace in his trunks. He opened the door to his bedroom and padded down the long, empty hallway, following the red carpet and the row of closed bedroom doors until he came to the grand staircase. He could hear the faint noise of cheering, but he saw no one when he glanced over the railing to the lobby. Taking the stairs down, he followed yet another long hallway until he came across an open door.

The sound of cheering grew louder, and as Ryon approached a drawing room, he glanced inside to see Fynn sitting alone in an armchair, watching a soccer game on the wall mounted TV. As usual, he was smoking. He wore the same clothes as last night—a black t-shirt, blue jeans, and brown boots. Had he gone to bed at all?

"Can't sleep either?" Ryon asked as he walked into the room.

Fynn's eyes darted to Ryon before he shook his head and inhaled from his cigarette. He pointed to the TV. "Did you know there's a twenty-four-hour soccer station? We didn't have this at the manor. Maybe joining the King here at the palace isn't such a bad thing after all."

Ryon snorted. Trust Fynn to find something positive in a bad situation. Ryon glanced around the room. The walls were a dark mahogany like the wardrobe in his room and the carpet, the same red. A full-sized pool table sat at the back of the room beside a small bar that appeared to be fully stocked with different whiskey bottles. Vampires didn't do regular meals. They were fine as long as they had blood once a night, but anything else was just for enjoyment, like alcohol. Striding over to the small bar, Ryon poured himself two glasses of whiskey. He took up the armchair beside Fynn and handed him a drink.

Together, they sat in silence, drinking and watching as the soccer ball was kicked from one player to the next before a chorus of cheers erupted, signalling that someone had scored a goal.

"Have you seen Kove?" Ryon asked without taking his eyes off the TV.

"Not since the meal last night." There was a pause as Fynn took a long drag of his smoke. "Why can't you sleep?"

Ryon scrubbed a hand over his face and sighed. "A lot on my mind I guess."

Fynn tapped his ashes onto the ash tray that sat on the coffee table between them. "Does this have anything to do with that human woman you bolted out of the manor for last night?"

"Maybe."

"Careful Ryon," Fynn warned before he took a sip of the whiskey. "Getting too involved with a human is risky business. Does Kove know about it? Is that why he's got his back up?"

When Ryon downed his whiskey in one shot, Fynn chuckled. "I'll take that as a yes." Fynn's smile faded, and he looked to Ryon. "I mean it, be careful. There's a reason Kove hates humans so much."

Ryon sat up, his eyes wide. "You know what happened to him?"

Fynn shrugged. "It's not my story to tell. All I'm saying is, just be wary about mixing emotions and humans."

Ryon's lips thinned as he considered what could have happened to Kove to make him so hateful. Then he shook his head. "Regardless, I don't get what any of this has to do with Kove. My decisions are none of his business."

"True," Fynn agreed with a nod. "But Kove is protective...

to a fault. And I'm sure whatever his problem is and whatever he's trying to do, it's because he's trying to protect you from getting hurt."

Ryon wasn't so sure about that, but he kept that thought to himself. He let the silence stretch out between them before he said, "I'm going to try Soran again." Ryon had tried to call Soran last night, but it had gone straight to voicemail each time. Pulling out the phone he'd shoved into the pocket of his slacks, he dialled Soran...only for it to go to voicemail yet again. He shook his head. "Still nothing." Throwing the phone onto the table beside his drink, he sighed and sat back. "The King is hiding something. I don't know what, but he is."

Fynn nodded as he took another deep puff of his cigarette, letting the smoke billow out of his mouth and filling the room with the tobacco scent. *Fuck it.* Ryon leaned across and gestured for Fynn to hand over the cigarette. Fynn lifted a brow but didn't protest as he handed it over. Ryon wasn't a smoker, but he needed something to do right now, and smoking may as well be it. He inhaled deeply as Fynn replaced the smoke, pulling out a new one. Leaning back in his chair, Ryon lifted his scarred hand, put the cigarette between his lips and ran his finger over the back of the scars.

"You know, you never did tell me how you got that," Fynn asked, pointing the smoke at Ryon's hand.

Ryon shrugged. "That's because I don't know. It must have been when I was a human though, or I would have healed. It's strange, I've been having this dream lately where I was a young vampire and reached out into the sunlight, getting these scars." He shook his head. "It felt so real."

Fynn scoffed and took another puff of his smoke. "Young vampire? Really?"

Ryon couldn't help but chuckle. "I know. Ridiculous, right?" Humans were transitioned into Vampires as adults because, if it was even attempted on a child or adolescent, they wouldn't survive the transition. Or at least that was what Ryon had heard.

"I keep having a reoccurring dream too," Fynn said, snapping Ryon's attention back to him. Fynn's gaze had dropped, and he seemed to be lost in his own thoughts.

"What's it about?"

Fynn blinked, seemingly pulling himself out of where he'd drifted to, and inhaled from the cigarette again. "It doesn't matter."

Ryon nodded, inhaling from his own cigarette. He could understand not wanting to talk and he'd respect that. Changing the subject, he glanced around and asked, "you feel like doing some exploring?"

It only took a moment for Fynn to answer. "Why not," he said as he downed his drink in one gulp and turned off the TV.

Ryon leaned forward and put out the cigarette on the ash tray, waiting until Fynn did the same. Closing the door to the drawing room behind them, Ryon and Fynn stepped out into the hallway.

"So, you're not gonna see the human again, are you?" Fynn asked as they walked to nowhere in particular. Ryon was barefoot, but Fynn's boots thudded with each step as they passed a few closed doors.

Ryon pursed his lips together. "You're sounding a lot like Kove right about now."

Fynn just shrugged in response. They kept walking until they reached the grand staircase and decided to head down to the ground level. They entered the lobby area by the entrance, and with no idea where they were going, they started down the opposite hallway. "Hey, I ain't judging you, man. But considering your species are about to go to war with hers, don't you think she'd be safer without you around?"

"I'll protect her."

Fynn lifted a brow. "From the King? I'm pretty sure his Royal Highness won't appreciate one of his men cavorting with a human when his ultimate goal is to destroy them all."

Ryon stopped in his tracks and prepared to argue with Fynn when the sound of voices echoed down the hall. Their heads turned in unison at the sound, and that was when Ryon noticed two steel swinging doors at the end of the hallway.

"Is that a kitchen?" Fynn asked.

"Sure, looks like it," Ryon answered, leading the way.

The doors burst open as a small male in a suit emerged carrying a tray. Ryon's gaze dipped to the tray and noticed an empty gold chalice like what they had drank from last night... and a hypodermic needle and tube. He recalled the way the blood had tasted fresh, too fresh to not be straight from the vein...*by using a hypodermic needle.* But where were the humans? Where were they getting the blood from?

"Oh!" the male said on a gasp, his brows lifting so high they almost met his hairline. He raised his spare hand to steady the tray that threatened to topple when the male had jumped. "Uh. Uh...Master Fynn and Master...Master..."

"Ryon," Ryon said.

The male's eyes widened briefly before they darted around the empty hallway. "Master *Ryon.* My apologies." The male bowed and then lifted his head, suddenly looking very nervous. "Is...is there anything I may help with?" his eyes flicked behind Ryon and Fynn before meeting their gazes once more. "King Drosera would prefer all guests remain in the upstairs rooms."

Really? Now it was Ryon's turn to raise his brows.

"If you don't mind, I must deliver this and then I will return to guide you back to your rooms? Or...or if you'd prefer, I can give you a tour of the palace? The library is on the second floor, and it is quite spectacular."

Ryon's gaze flicked to Fynn. "Ah, no, that's fine. We'll let you make your..." he glanced at the tray, "...*delivery*. We can find our own way back to our rooms. Thank you."

"Yes...Yes, master." With another bow, the small male rushed off down the hallway and up the grand staircase, leaving them alone once again.

"What the hell was he doing with a needle?" Ryon whispered to Fynn as he watched the male disappear, but Fynn's gaze was locked on something at the end of the hall.

"What's that?" Fynn asked, making Ryon turn around. There was another door, right at the end of the hallway and off to the side. It was a large wooden door that was painted white like the walls, so it would have been easy to overlook it if not for the round black handle.

"Maybe it's the reason the King would prefer all guests remain upstairs," Ryon said flatly, walking forward. He heard Fynn behind him as they approached the door. Ryon reached for the handle, and with one last glance down the hallway— ensuring it was still empty—Ryon turned it, surprised to find it was unlocked.

He pushed the door open wider and was met with a dark staircase, lit only by a sconce lamp at the base of the stairs. Unlike the grand staircase, this wasn't grand at all. It was steel and spiralled down in a tight circle to another hallway. Ryon glanced back at Fynn, but words didn't need to be exchanged. Fynn nodded, and Ryon turned to descend the staircase with Fynn following closely behind. When his bare feet touched the cold stone floor, a ripple of apprehension ran through him. What was down here? Call it curiosity, call it due diligence, but they *needed* to see what was here. If the King was hiding something, they should know what.

As they reached the base of the staircase, that sconce lamp —and the others just like it that lined the hallway—automatically turned on in succession. And what looked to be a very long hallway made of aged sandstone was lit up. While the rest of the palace looked somewhat modern and luxurious, this hallway looked straight out of a medieval history book. The spaced-out lights along the hallway cast shadows on the walls, but it looked like there were drawings...or was it writing?... along the wall about halfway down.

"This is fucking creepy," Fynn said unhelpfully.

Ryon didn't turn back to his friend. Instead, he walked to where the markings were on the wall and ran his hand over the engraved etchings. He was wrong. They weren't drawings or writings. They were names. Rows and rows of etched names.

Vincente Drosera
Alec Drosera
Kayne Drosera
Dorlus Drosera

The names went on and on. Column after column and row after row.

"Names of the Royal blood line," Ryon said absent-mindedly.

"It's a family tree?" Fynn asked, coming forward to stand beside Ryon.

Ryon followed the etchings further down the hall until he found the name of the current King—Cazimir Drosera. He heard the familiar 'ding' of a text message on both his phone and Fynn's, but he didn't take his eyes from the wall as he frowned and leaned closer.

"It's from Zane. The King is calling us all into a meeting right now to talk about his plans for tonight. Apparently, there's some human gala event tonight, and he wants to..." Ryon stopped listening to Fynn as he frowned down at the wall of names. And more specifically, the name *underneath* King Cazimir Drosera.

"Since when did King Cazimir have a son?" Ryon asked, interrupting Fynn.

"What?" Fynn's tone suggested he was just as confused as Ryon felt. "He doesn't. We'd know about it if there was a prince. Hell, there's not even a Queen."

"Then why is there a name right here underneath his own? Look, it says right here," Ryon pointed to the last etching.

Ryszard Drosera.

CHAPTER EIGHTEEN

Your parents would be so proud of you.
Wendy's words repeated in Laina's mind as she drove home after the meeting. The logo brief had taken no more than half an hour, but then Wendy had asked Laina if she wanted to see the handmade quilts and...well, Laina couldn't say no. The quilt showcase turned into a house tour, which turned into another cup of tea and more chocolate-chip cookies. All in all, Laina had stayed another couple of hours until the sun began to set. And despite all the things they had talked about, the same words were stuck in her mind. *Your parents would be so proud of you*. Would they be proud of her? For almost sleeping with a vampire? *No*. No, of course not. They'd be rolling in their graves with disappointment. And that thought made her want to double over with the pain of her grief.

As she continued to drive, she fought the urge to scroll through her contacts and call her father—it was their thing to call each other on long drives. Or at least, it used to be. And she longed to sit down with her mother and talk over coffee like they used to. *God*, she missed them. She missed the way her father used to call her his little girl, even though she was almost as tall as him. She missed the way her mother used to remind her not to slouch, that she would end up with a curved spine one day because of it. Both of those things used to drive Laina insane. She'd hated it. But now, she would do absolutely anything for them to do it again.

Ten minutes later, Laina pulled into the car park of her apartment, still in a daze of chaotic thoughts and memories. She made her way upstairs to her apartment and dropped her bag by the door. She stood there for long moments, feeling more lost than ever before. Last night she'd told Ryon about her parents. She'd let down her guard, and despite what happened with Ryon afterwards, it had opened up a pandora's box of emotions. And then speaking to Wendy about them...It was like reopening old wounds that never quite healed. Her heart was flipping between numbing emptiness and agonising grief. She thought she had processed this. She thought she was done with the pain...but it still felt as raw as if it had happened yesterday.

Laina's gaze drifted to her bedroom. After her parent's death, Brynn had given her a box of items from that night, believing it would bring her 'closure'. Laina had never opened it, and Brynn had never asked for it back. The word 'closure' itself was so final. It was the end. It meant accepting what happened and acknowledging that nothing could bring them back. She knew they were gone, and she had, in fact, accepted that. But had she dealt with it? She had to admit, that was a big fat no. For the last six months, she had avoided thinking about the future at all costs. Thinking about the future meant accepting that her parents would never be a part of it. And maybe now was the time.

Walking through the dim living area, she made her way to the bedroom, where she turned on the light and opened the wardrobe. Reaching up on her tiptoes, she pulled down a box from the top shelf and stepped back to sit on the end of her bed. A wave of nausea rolled through Laina, but she took a deep breath and steeled herself. The thought that her parents were one of the last to touch these items made her chest tighten. It was like tearing open stitches that barely held a gaping wound closed. The grief exploded in Laina's chest as tears didn't so much prick her eyes as pour from them.

Swiping away to clear her blurry vision, Laina forced her fingers to move, lifting the lid of the cardboard box and placing it on the bed. Looking inside, she took in what she saw. A plain white envelope, a small black clutch that she recognised as her mother's, and her father's brown wallet that was too full of cards to close. The edges of her mouth lifted in a smile. Her father was a stickler for a good reward system and loved to collect stamp cards. She lifted the brown wallet out of the box and placed it on her bed. Her mother's clutch was empty, the usual contents now scattered at the bottom of the box—her phone, keys, and a pale pink lipstick that she loved. Her father's phone was missing, but he'd left it at home that particular night, so no doubt Brynn had packed it away with all their other belongings when she had cleaned out their house.

Laina reached for her mother's mobile and held it to her chest. She recalled all the conversations she'd had with her over upgrading the damn thing but still, her mother had insisted on keeping it. It wasn't a smartphone or anything, but since her mother had no social media accounts, it wasn't a problem for her.

After taking a deep breath, Laina held her finger down over the power button. She didn't even know if it was charged, and come to think of it, it may not turn on at all. However, the logo that suddenly appeared told her otherwise. The 'Ping' of a message notification rang out once...then twice...three times... then four. The sound went on and on until Laina lost count. Her stomach twisted as the sound, whilst still so familiar, now felt foreign without her mother in the room. She considered reading the texts as she stared at the phone. Should she be doing this? Was this a violation of her mother's privacy? Or would this truly give her some form of closure?

With trembling fingers, Laina unlocked the phone with a swipe—her mother didn't believe in using pin-codes for phones—and frowned when she saw that the last text was from Brynn. She swallowed hard and hesitated for a moment before opening the text message.

Mum, I must be going crazy sending a text to you knowing you'll never be able to read it. I just don't know what else to do. It's been a month now, and I miss you so Goddamn much. I still can't believe you're gone. Laina is struggling. Or at least I think she is. I don't know. She won't tell me anything. She won't talk to me. She won't open up, and I don't know how to help her. This is something you were so good at. You always had a way to help us whenever we were down. But I'm not you, Mum, and I don't know how to be. It's like she's just completely shut me out, and I... I feel so alone. God, I miss you.

Brynn x

Laina re-read that same message three more times before she sat back. She swallowed hard as the guilt crept in. She'd been so selfish that she hadn't stopped to think of how Brynn might be feeling. Brynn had become this overprotective parent figure which had driven Laina to push her away...but she had done it all to try to help Laina. At the outset, Brynn and Laina's relationship seemed perfectly normal. Still, deep down, the elephant in the room was now the size of a house. Brynn thought she could be there for Laina by being a mother figure when what Laina truly needed was a sister. But what about Brynn? The guilt inside Laina doubled, tripled, as she realised she hadn't even tried to be there for Brynn.

Laina closed the message and froze when she saw one of the last read texts. It was from *her*. As the tears pricked her eyes, she bit her bottom lip to keep from crying. She didn't need to open it to know what it said, but she did anyway.

Hey Mum, won't be able to make it tonight to dinner as we're going out. Love you guys x

It was such a casual text...and it was the last thing she ever said to her mother.

Laina heard a faint ringing sound, and she frowned, looking down at the phone in confusion. It took her a moment to realise the sound was, in fact, coming from *her* phone outside. She wiped away her tears, turned off her mother's phone and hurriedly packed it into the box along with all the other contents. She held the box to her chest once more before putting it back on the top shelf of her wardrobe. When she heard her phone ringing again, she rushed outside and fished through her bag to find it. It was Max.

"Hey Max," Laina said, scrubbing a hand over her face to compose herself.

"Hey, you!" Max's bubbly voice came back at her. His tone then grew serious, "Are you okay?" *Observant, as always.*

"Yeah, I'm fine, just...fell asleep for a minute," she replied, hoping he believed her.

"That's a great idea, since it might be a late one tonight," Max said, the hint of a smile in his voice. *What?* "I know how long it can take you to get ready, so I figured I'd give you a heads up. I'll be picking you up in twenty minutes."

Confused, she frowned. "For what?"

Silence. "...the gala?" There was no hint of a smile this time. "You, uh...you said you'd come with me?"

Laina's stomach twisted at the disappointment in his tone, and she suddenly felt bad for forgetting. "Ha!" The word exploded from her mouth, not knowing what else to say. "Got you!" She sang out, hoping Max fell for it. And by the sound of the sigh on the other end of the line, he did. "I'll meet you downstairs in twenty minutes, okay?"

"Well, eighteen now," Max chuckled.

Shit. "See you soon!"

"And don't forget it's black tie!"

Double shit.

Laina dropped her phone and ran into her room, pulling open the wardrobe. It took two minutes to pick an outfit—the floor-length strappy black dress with the plunging neckline and back that she'd bought for her design school graduation party. Besides the fact that it was a stunning dress, it was also the only thing she owned that was even remotely classified as black tie.

She rushed into the shower, not waiting for the water to warm up before she got in and began washing her hair. She would normally hate that, but the cool water was refreshing. It made her feel better, temporarily washing away all the thoughts and emotions from earlier.

Ten minutes later, she was dried and dressed. There was no time to straighten or style her hair like usual. She'd just have to let it dry naturally into a mix of waves and curls. She threw on some makeup, attempting the smoky eye look, before finishing it off with some red lipstick. In the rush of getting ready, she hoped she pulled off the 'sexy' look and didn't lean more into the 'hooker' category. Digging through the bottom of the wardrobe, she found some black strappy heels to match and packed her phone, wallet, and keys into a black clutch. *Done.* Laina rushed out of her apartment and outside to see Max sitting in his car, looking at the time on his wristwatch.

"Sorry! Sorry!" she said, getting into his car and hoping she didn't accidentally expose herself from the low-cut V that sat between her breasts. She pulled on her seatbelt and turned to see Max looking back at her with wide eyes. "What?" She glanced down—*nope, nothing exposed.* "Is this okay?"

Max's gaze seemed to dip down to her toes before slowly making his way back up. "More than okay. You look..." she saw his Adam's apple bob before he finished, "you look beautiful."

She gave him a half smile, suddenly remembering that she didn't want his attention in *that* way. "Thank you." She had to admit, Max didn't look half bad in his black tux either. But he was no Ryon. *Dammit.* She didn't want to think about Ryon right now. She *wouldn't.*

The edges of Max's lips lifted as he smiled in return. *Did he move closer?* His gaze lingered on her eyes, too long for it to not to be awkward. For *her* at least. He, on the other hand, seemed to be perfectly comfortable. His eyes seemed to grow heavy-lidded before that grey gaze darted down to her lips. *Oh no.*

"So," Laina said abruptly, "this gala..." she let the words linger between them until his low lashes lifted and he pulled back.

Max let out a sigh and ran a hand through his hair. He nodded and sent her a smile that looked far from genuine. Had he read the room? Had he *finally* read the room?

"So, what's this gala for again?" she asked, knowing exactly what it was for but wanting to break through that awkward silence.

"Apparently, it's a big deal. And turns out it's not just a design thing either. It's meant to be a 'celebration of the arts'," Max said, resting his hands on the steering wheel as he used his fingers to emphasise the name. "It's open to designers, artists, entertainers...basically anyone employed in the creative industries around town. It's the biggest event that Ladwick has seen in years. You don't see me as more than a friend, do you?"

Laina blinked. Max had added that question at the end there so smoothly, it caught her off guard. "I-I, uh..."

Max sighed. "It's okay, Laina. I thought maybe you...I assumed you felt the same. But if you don't, just tell me and I won't say anything more about it."

Laina bit her bottom lip, considering what to say. She decided honesty was best. "I'm sorry, Max. I...I don't."

Max nodded gravely. After a moment he asked, "can we still be friends at least?"

The relief that coursed through Laina had her letting her head fall back against the headrest. She looked back at him, meeting his gaze with a smile. "Yes. Of course."

"Thank God," Max said with a sigh. He started the car. "Well, are you ready to go to a gala?"

Laina's smile widened, and she leaned over to gently place

a reassuring hand over Max's still bandaged one. "With my best friend? Absolutely."

Laina sunk back into the passenger seat and looked out the window as Max pulled out of the parking spot. After everything that had happened lately, she needed a distraction, and maybe this...gala was just the thing. She loved all things design and the creative arts, and even though a part of her wanted to curl up on her lounge at home, she was also excited to be surrounded by things she loved. *Yes*, tonight she'd let her hair down. She'd relax. And she'd enjoy the night with her best friend.

CHAPTER NINETEEN

Ryon looked up at where the King stood before them all on the grand staircase of his palace. Zane was by the King's side as usual, armed with his signature bow and arrow as the King continued to give his spiel to the Shadows below.

"This isn't about sending a message to the humans. This is *war*."

Ryon frowned. *War?* He glanced around at his fellow Shadow members. Fynn, Xavier, Malik, Rune, Damien, and Darick. They all looked slightly concerned but didn't tear their eyes from the King. Kove's jaw ticked with tension, but the determination on his face told Ryon he was completely and utterly onboard with the King's plan. And after what Fynn had said, Ryon wasn't surprised.

When Ryon caught the sudden scent of Reds, he turned around...to see row after row of the red-eyed vampires standing at the back of the room. His eyes flared with rage, and he prepared to unsheathe his sword when he heard the King's next words.

"And gentle males, I'd like to introduce you to..." Ryon

glanced back at the King to see him gesture to the Reds, "your battalion."

Ryon knew the moment the Shadows turned and saw what stood behind; Low curses sounded out around him. And from directly beside him, he heard Fynn mumble, "that's not good."

The Reds stood motionless as if frozen in time. Their scarlet eyes appeared almost glazed over as they stared blankly at the King as if awaiting instructions.

"Tonight, is the night," the King continued, dragging everyone's attention back to him. "Tonight, is the night that we start our assault and take back what is rightfully ours. *We* own the night!"

A chorus of "*we own the night!*" exploded from the back of the room, the Reds echoing the King's words. A shiver ran down Ryon's spine at the sound of it. It was like an echo of a thousand voices in unison, as if they were manufactured that way. *Wait.* He glanced back at the Reds...The way they their eyes were wide and glazed over as they locked on the King, the way they stood rigid and at the ready...

"They look like they're compelled," he whispered to no one.

"What?" Fynn's whispering voice came back to him.

He shook his head. "Nothing." He turned back to the King as he continued his speech. Even if those Reds were at the razor's edge of losing control, they couldn't be compelled —no vampire could.

"...and tonight, they will not only learn of our existence, but they will also learn to fear us!" The King's loud voice boomed around the large room. Now when Ryon looked at the King, he realised he wore no crown. His short black hair was slicked back, which only made his already hardened features stand out. His thick eyebrows were drawn low but not enough to restrict those golden eyes from boring into everyone as he spoke. He wore black trousers and a black shirt like he had last night, but now he donned a red velvet suit jacket with the Royal crest embroidered into his shoulder.

It was then that the situation sunk in. The King truly was starting a *war*. A war between vampires and humans. Like Soran, Ryon had never questioned the King before. Well, not *really*. After all, the last fifty years of his life had been spent enforcing the rules that the King created. But now, Ryon had to question whether the King had the best interest of the species or his own inflated ego at heart.

"As Zane mentioned to you all, there is a gala being held in Ladwick community hall. We will never have a better opportunity to show our presence and put the fear of their own God into those pitiful humans. We will never have a better opportunity to destroy so many of them. Whilst the event in the Ladwick hospital caused city-wide terror, it will be nothing compared to *tonight*."

The King took a step down and lifted one finger in the air. "There is one and *only* one rule tonight—Kill as many humans as possible. Bite them, stab them, compel them to kill themselves, rip their organs out of their frail bodies with your bare hands—I don't care how you do it. Just kill them!" As a chorus of cheers erupted at the back of the room, the King's gaze raked over everyone before falling directly on Ryon.

A tremor of pure panic rippled through Ryon as his thoughts immediately went to Laina. He hoped like hell she was at home, safe and sound. And nowhere near the Ladwick community hall.

CHAPTER TWENTY

Laina took a sip of her second—*or was it third?*—glass of champagne as she glanced around the Ladwick community hall. Her mother used to bring her to dancing lessons at one of the rooms here when she was about seven or eight years old. She remembered the way it always smelled musty, as if her dance classes were the only ones to have ever opened the doors and let some fresh air in. Now, however, there were no more individual rooms to be hired out for birthday parties or after-school activities. It had been renovated into one oversized and extravagant room that could host hundreds if not thousands of people—like tonight. And despite the Ladwick community hall being only a few blocks away from her apartment, she hadn't been inside since its renovation.

Another sip. Laina was well and truly feeling the buzz of the alcohol now as Max continued with the conversation around them. She wasn't a big drinker, but lately, her alcohol intake had increased dramatically. She was getting to like how it dimmed her thoughts and emotions, even if only for a little while. When Laina and Max first arrived, they were guided to a large table where Max's new colleagues sat. Their conversation began politely enough but quickly turned to office politics and gossip. That was when Laina found comfort in her glass of champagne to avoid the awkwardness.

She glanced up from her glass as the background jazz music seemed to quieten, making her wonder if the alcohol's effects made her hear things. Then the overhead lights dimmed, and she knew she didn't imagine it. The green 'exit' lights over the doors at both ends of the hall provided some illumination but not enough. She reached over and gripped Max's arm as apprehension grew inside her.

She felt Max's hand cover hers. "It's okay, it's just the award ceremony starting. They probably have some grand entrance planned. *Relax.*"

Laina let out the breath she didn't realise she'd been holding. Releasing Max's hand, she felt around in the dark for her champagne. She downed the rest of the contents as floodlights abruptly lit up the stage at the front of the room, and the low hum of chatter dissipated.

"See, I told you," Max whispered as a man with long midnight black hair stepped out onto the stage.

"Is that *velvet*?" Laina snickered as she poured herself another glass from the nearby bottle. The man on stage wore a red velvet suit jacket over a black shirt, black pants and strode confidently into the middle of the stage.

"Humans!" the man demanded, throwing his arms out in a grand gesture. The odd way he'd just addressed the room made Laina pause and any humour she felt vanished in an instant. *Humans?* "Welcome to your...*demise*!" The man onstage enunciated the last word by pulling his lips back on a snarl. And that was when Laina saw...his *fangs*.

The icy dread of fear rushed through her, freezing her in place as any alcohol in her system vanished. That happy buzz from minutes ago turned into sheer terror as she realised the man on stage was a vampire—and from the way he dressed and the authority he oozed—he was likely some kind of leader.

"We have to go," Laina whisper-yelled to Max, her heart thumping so wildly that it felt as though it would explode at any minute. "We have to leave. *Now.*"

"What are you talking about?" Max leaned closer to her. "Will you relax? This is all part of the show."

Laina heard the sound of doors exploding open, followed immediately by chairs dragging and panicked screams as people stood from their tables. The man on stage began to laugh maniacally, a contrast to the panicking people around her. *What's going on?*

"Can you see anything?" Laina yelled over the shrieks to Max. She stood from the table, her eyes peeled wide as she glanced around frantically to see what was happening.

Max stood from his chair, taking Laina's hand and squeezing it tightly as the rest of his colleagues got to their feet. The spotlights remained on the stage, but the rest of the hall was still blanketed in almost darkness, casting eery shadows around them.

Laina's breaths quickened as she glanced between the two exits—or at least in their direction, since people were blocking the way for her to see the actual doors. The terror coursing through her threatened to send her to the ground in tears but she clenched her fists tightly and steeled herself to remain standing. Just like Ryon had pointed out last night, after everything she'd witnessed, she wasn't rocking in a corner somewhere—she was still standing. And unlike everyone else in this room, she knew the truth about vampires.

Inhaling deeply, Laina ignored her shallow breaths and her racing heart and stepped onto her chair, getting a higher vantage-point so that she could see what was happening. From the silhouettes and the moving shadows, she could see people...fighting? She swung around to the opposite exit to see more people brawling and running in all directions—even over the tabletops—to get *away* from both exits.

"What are you doing?" Max yelled up at her, but she ignored it, going on her tiptoes to see—*Oh, God.* Her heart stopped when her gaze landed on the people—*no, the vampires* —piling *into* the room and attacking.

"They've blocked the exits," she rushed out, glancing around frantically for another door. Another exit. *The stage.* She swung back towards the stage—the man, or *male*, in the red velvet suit was now on the floor, his mouth over a woman's neck as other people ran away from him. She swallowed down the cry of fear and continued to search around the stage. Surely there was a stage door somewhere...*There*—

Laina screamed as the chair she was standing on got knocked. She toppled backwards but Max's strong arms caught her, steadying her back down on the floor. Her breaths were ragged as she reminded herself that she was still alive. She was still alive and still standing. But in the thirty seconds she'd been on the chair, more and more people had rushed towards their table, gathering in the middle of the room in a chaotic bid to get away from the exits.

"Stage door!" she yelled out to Max over the deafening screams. "We need to get to the stage door!"

"Get under the table!" one of Max's colleagues shouted from behind them as a fresh wave of people charged towards them, screaming, and crying out.

Laina didn't have time to process any of it before Max yanked her arm and dragged her across to the next table. And the table after that. He pulled her down under it and barely made it there before the stampede of people in black tie knocked into them.

"Vampires! Vampires!" a man in a tux yelled out as he ran past.

"Did he say *vampires?*" Max asked from beside her, making her glance over at him. His brows were drawn low in confusion, his eyes darting around the room. His gaze seemed to lock on something in front of them, his eyes going wide before he let out a curse, followed by the word again. "*Vampires.*"

Laina could barely hear Max over the screams and the echo of her own racing heart, but she'd caught the word clearly enough and when she followed his line of sight, she knew he'd pieced it all together.

A woman in a navy ballgown was striding past, oblivious of everything around her. The woman didn't run. She didn't even rush. Instead, she walked slowly as if going for a quiet stroll through the park. The woman's eyes were peeled wide, hair was half pulled out of a styled updo, and blood seeped from...two twin puncture wounds at her neck. Her eyes dipped to the woman's arms which she held outstretched in front of her. Each wrist showed the same two holes. They dripped with blood, running down her hands, onto the formal dress and leaving a trail of crimson behind her.

The breath caught in Laina's throat at the horror of the

scene before her, but then she steeled herself to get a grip. This wasn't a surprise. She knew vampires existed, and she needed to get past that and get to the stage door.

"We need to get to the stage," she repeated, leaning into Max's ear so he could hear her. "There's a door beside it that should lead us out."

She turned and, seeing a gap through the crowds of frenzied people, she took Max's hand, pulling him out from the table. Not letting go, Laina lifted her dress up with her free hand and ran as fast as her stilettos would carry her over to the next table. They squatted below it just as Laina felt the thud of someone falling on top of it. She gasped as a woman rolled off the table and onto the floor in front of them. Max let out a string of curses as Laina put her hand over her mouth. The woman's throat was...was no longer there. *Oh my God.*

Fighting back the bile creeping up her throat, she turned to Max and pointed to the stage. "We need to get there." His eyes darted to where she was pointing. After a moment, he looked back at her and nodded in understanding.

They waited there for what felt like forever as more and more people—more and more *bodies*—were thrown about like rag dolls to the soundtrack of deafening screams. Hundreds of injured and dead bodies began to litter the floor, while hundreds more continued to run around in a mixed state of frenzied panic and calm shock. Laina unstrapped her shoes and took them off, placing them behind her as if she didn't want anyone to trip over them. *Yeah, like that is concern right now.*

When she spotted a lull in the movement of people, she took Max's hand and rushed forward. She ran as fast as she could, squeezing Max's hand more with each step. They passed one table, then the next. More people were down this end now, running in every direction and almost blocking their path. But they were almost there. *Almost there.* Just two more tab—

Max's hand was suddenly ripped from her grasp.

She halted and swung around. *Where is he? Where is he?* She spotted him through the hordes of people rushing around her and knocking into her. A man—*no, a vampire*—had him pinned down on a table, hovering over his neck.

Terror shot through her as she pushed her way through the crowd and dug her nails into the vampire's shoulders, yanking back as hard as she could. *Nothing.* Nothing happened. She threw her weight behind it and tried again. *Nothing.* Her eyes landed on the bottle of wine on the table beside her and without a second thought, she reached for it— glad to see the lid still on it—turning it around, she smashed it into the back of the vampire's head. Max kicked out, sending the unsuspecting vampire stumbling sideways.

Laina and Max froze as the vampire hissed, his red eyes flaring with rage as he reached for his now bleeding head. Would he retaliate? Would he kill them? *Shit. Shit. Shit.* But then the vampire lifted his nose into the air and swung around to where the woman with the bleeding neck and wrists was still stumbling around. Laina's relief was short lived, replaced by a wave of guilt as the vampire launched himself on the woman, taking her down to the floor.

"Laina!"

It was Max. She tore her eyes from the vampire and the woman on the floor to see Max get caught up in a horde of people that had rushed from the opposite side of the room. *Fuck!*

"Max!" she sprinted forward but stopped when she could no longer see him. *Fuck!* "Max!" she called out as people bumped into her and pushed past her. *Where is he? Where is he?*

"Funny seeing you here." That voice made Laina halt. "Looks like I don't have to worry about wiping your memory after all." Her whole body tensed as she slowly turned around.

Her stomach plummeted to the floor as her gaze landed on the rugged, broad-shouldered man—*male*—before her. He still donned the leather pants, a black t-shirt, and the leather jacket with the ribbed sleeves. His hair was pulled back in a bun, and his golden eyes were blazing with fire as they locked on her. The breath caught in her throat as she watched the male who'd been in her apartment last night reach behind and unsheathe the sword at his back. *Oh God. Oh God. Oh God.*

She glanced behind her but still couldn't see Max. A small whimper left her as she wondered if he'd been attacked like that woman on the ground. She swallowed hard and looked back to the vampire before her, knowing she had no hope of fighting him off or evading his next move. Her heart caught in her throat and her lungs were suddenly void of oxygen as she stood, frozen and unmoving as he lowered his chin. Those golden eyes glared at her with a hate she couldn't understand as he lifted the sword and pointed the sharp blade directly at her. She opened her mouth to scream but with no air left in her lungs, no sound would come. He pulled back his lips on a snarl, exposing his sharp, white fangs.

And then he lunged.

CHAPTER TWENTY-ONE

After the King finished making his speech back at the manor, everyone followed him by fading to the Ladwick Community Hall. While Ryon had struggled with the moral implications of what he was expected to do—and if he was prepared to follow through with it—the King had instructed the Reds to go in first. Kove, however, was a different story. Against the King's order for the Shadows to wait, he ran head-long with the Reds, to be one of the first into the hall.

"Let's go," Malik called out as the hundreds of Reds disappeared into the building. It was their turn. Ryon could feel that the others were just as apprehensive and hesitant as he was, as they stepped forward. They entered the lobby area to the sounds of screams, and when they stepped into the hall, chaos erupted around them. The scent of blood, death, and fear were rampant, and Ryon had to steel himself to keep walking.

"This...this is wrong," Fynn said softly from behind him. "This is so wrong." The words cut through the noise and horror around them and seemed to strike at Ryon's very soul. Fynn had voiced the same words that had been running through Ryon's mind. It *was* wrong. Everything about this situation was wrong. The large hall was bathed in darkness, the only light reflecting around the room came from the spotlights on the stage...but it was enough to highlight the gruesome scene before him.

The King had been right when he said what happened at the hospital last night would be nothing compared to *this*. Some humans were running, some screaming, and others were silent as they walked around in a daze. And then there were the dead. So many dead. The Reds had only been inside the hall for mere minutes, and yet the damage they had caused had been staggering. Bodies lay strewn across tabletops, chairs, and the floor, all wearing formal outfits heavily stained in a crimson colour. The Reds didn't have swords like the Shadows, but they did just fine with their speed and fangs.

"B...Benjamin? Ben?" A woman appeared out of nowhere, stumbling into Ryon as she called out for someone. Ryon caught her before she fell, steadying her on her feet as she glanced up at him. Her hair was falling out of a formal bun atop of her head, her eyes were wide, and her skin was a pale grey covered in a fine sheen of sweat.

His eyes lowered to the four—*or six?*—twin punctures at her neck that bled freely, pouring down her neckline and soaking the navy ballgown she wore. A knot formed in Ryon's throat. More than one vampire had taken from her, and they'd all just left her to bleed out.

"H-have you seen B-Benjamin? We need to go h-home. I... I left the stove on. I n-need to turn it off. We have to get h-home."

Ryon was suddenly aware of the woman's trembling form under his fingertips. He didn't need to check her pulse to know that her heart rate was slow and erratic. It wouldn't be long now.

"Shhh," Ryon said, aware of how absurd it was to say amidst the deafening madness surrounding them.

The woman quietened, her legs giving out under her. Ryon caught her and guided her down to the floor, placing her back against the door they'd just come in from. He felt the Shadows eyes on him, and he glanced over to see them watching him intently. He was momentarily surprised that they hadn't charged into the hall as per the King's instructions, but he could see the same conflict on their faces that he felt deep down.

Turning back to the woman, he knelt beside her and took her head in his hands. "You and Ben will be going home soon. You don't need to worry about the stove. You didn't leave it on." The woman visibly relaxed as Ryon's compulsion crept into her mind. "You're going to sleep now, and you won't feel anything else."

The woman's eyes closed as Ryon pulled his hands back and stood. And at that moment, the world seemed to stop. The cries and panicked screams dulled into silence. The movement around him halted as he looked around at the hollow, scarlet-coloured eyes of the Reds, the fierce determination on their faces as they bit, tore, and clawed at the helpless humans. Then he looked to the humans. To the terrified expressions on their faces as they ran or futilely attempted to fight back, and then to the soulless bodies of the dead. It wouldn't take long for word to spread about this, and the humans would come for them when it did. Ladwick was small compared to other towns in the Garabitha region—humans would gather. They would gather and they would find a way to kill them, starting with the vampires in Ladwick. The King wanted to come here tonight to send a powerful message that vampires were to be feared, and in a way, he was right. Vampires may be feared for their compulsion, ability to fade, and incredible strength. But humans had the day.

Ryon's gaze lifted to the stage where the King stood smiling at the chaos before him, dried blood covering his mouth and chin. From somewhere in the depths of his subconscious, Ryon heard the woman's words from what he had thought were his dreams.

You're better than this.

He didn't know why, but those words meant something to Ryon. He *was* better than this. Ryon was better than killing hundreds of humans just to send a message of fear.

"I can't do it," he said to no one. The world descended into chaos again as the scenes around him sped up, and the screams and cries grew deafening once more.

He glanced over at the Shadows, who stared at him as if he was the one with the instructions. "I..." his voice trailed off as he caught the scent of something sweet. Like...like...vanilla, cinnamon and...rose. He tensed with the realisation.

Laina. Laina was here.

Ryon swung around, looking frantically between the panicked humans. The scent was all but gone now, and he suddenly wondered if he'd imagined the whole thing up. But then his feet started moving of their own accord as if drawn to something on the other side of the room. He started running through the hordes of frenzied people, over bodies and pushing through the Reds and humans alike as his instinct beckoned him to the right-hand side of the stage.

And then he saw her.

He stopped abruptly when, between the crowds of people, he saw Laina standing two tables away. She wore a black dress with no back. As his gaze followed the curves of her figure and the hollow of her spine to the start of the material above her tailbone, he knew without a shadow of a doubt it was her. Movement caught his eye from somewhere in front of Laina, and his gaze darted to—

Kove. It was Kove. Kove was standing before her, his lips lifted on a snarl and his arm outstretched with his sword, the end of that sharp blade pointed right at Laina. *What the fuck is he doing?* Ryon hissed and exploded into a dead run, pushing people out of the way as he went. He could see Kove's eyes narrowed and locked on Laina, poised on the verge of thrusting that sword forward and through her very chest. *I'm not going to make it. Fuck, I'm not going to make it!*

At the very last second, Ryon closed his eyes and focused on fading to Laina. He hoped like hell his body would calm down enough to concentrate and make it happen. His entire being was thrumming with adrenalin, his mind flipping between fear for Laina and anger at Kove...but then, between one step to the next, it happened.

He opened his eyes to see...that he hadn't made it—not far enough. He appeared just behind Laina, and one glance at Kove told him she was seconds away from being struck in the heart. Ryon didn't waste another moment. Without hesitation, he pushed her out of the way—just as Kove's sword penetrated his chest.

CHAPTER TWENTY-TWO

I t all happened so fast. One second, Laina was staring down the blade of Kove's sword. The next, she was shoved to the side, catching herself on the nearby table. What just happened? She lifted a hand to her neck, to her chest, to her stomach. When she felt nothing, she straightened and looked down—nothing. No pain. No blood. No stab wound. She swung around, and her breath hitched at what she saw. It was *him*. It was Ryon... and Kove's hand held the sword jutting from Ryon's chest.

She watched in horror as his powerful body swayed. All the anger she held for him from last night evaporated as a wave of dread washed over her. He looked down, seemingly stunned for a moment before he placed his hands over Kove's on the hilt. Laina saw a muscle tick in Ryon's jaw before he guided Kove to yank it out of him, eliciting a gasp out of her.

And Kove appeared just as shocked. He held the sword by his side for a long moment, his wide eyes darting between Ryon and the wound. Kove's mouth opened and closed...and opened and closed. His expression was one of pure remorse, something she didn't think he was even capable of feeling. She watched as he slowly sheathed the sword on his back and then...vanished. Just *vanished*.

Laina swung around, but Ryon was already beside her, his body swaying slightly. He placed his hands on either side of her face, and for a moment, she wasn't sure if it was to comfort her or to hold himself up.

"You're okay," he said on a breath, the relief clear in his voice. "You're okay."

"My God, Ryon. You were *stabbed*!" She pulled back as her gaze darted to the long slit on his black t-shirt that now seeped with blood from the open wound underneath.

"I'll be okay," he said, releasing her. "But we need to get you out of here."

Max. "Max..." she started, her voice cracking as she glanced around Ryon. "We have to find Max!"

He stepped back but not before his brows drew together. "*He's* here?"

"Yes, he brought me here," she answered absentmindedly as she glanced from person to person, looking for him. Where is he?

Laina felt Ryon's hand on her arm. "There's no time, you need to get out of here," his tone brooked no argument, but she wasn't going anywhere without Max.

"Laina!"

Max. She pulled away from Ryon and swung around just as Max enveloped her in a bone-breaking embrace. *Thank God.*

She pulled back from the embrace, feeling Ryon's intense stare on her as she assessed Max. He had a cut on his forehead, his hair was tussled, his tux skewed, and his shirt half torn at the base...but he was okay. *He's okay.*

Max seemed to notice Ryon in that moment. He tensed, his body turning towards Ryon as he slowly stepped in front of Laina protectively. "Laina...get behind me," he said low, as if trying not to make any sudden movements.

"Max, it's not—" she began but was cut off when Ryon moved impossibly fast, suddenly appearing right in front of Max with his lip pulled back on a snarl as he stood over him. *Shit!* "Ryon!" she called, stepping out from behind Max.

"Come between us again and I'll feed you to the rabid vampires in this room," Ryon's voice was low, threatening.

Laina froze, unsure whether Max would argue and unsure if Ryon would follow through. She glanced over at Max, he was pale-faced and wide-eyed, but she was relieved when he slowly nodded. It was then that Laina realised something. She could hear Ryon. *Clearly.* She glanced over her shoulder. The scenes were still chaotic with people frantically running everywhere, but the screams weren't as deafening anymore. And she knew why. The floor of the hall was littered—*littered*—with bodies.

"Let's go," Ryon said, dragging her attention away from the horrific scenes.

"There's a side door," Laina said, quickly. "By the stage. There should be a way out from there."

Ryon glanced over to the stage and then the door. "Stay close," he said to her, and then, as if to make sure she'd do just that, he took her hand. Laina didn't fight it. In fact, a comforting warmth rippled through her at the touch of his skin against hers and she had the fleeting thought that she was safe now that he was here. Ryon led her through the crowd until they made it to the table closest to the stage where the door was. He halted, tugging Laina down beside him under the table as Max followed suit.

Laina turned to gauge how far they were from that door when, in the reflections of the spotlights on stage, she saw a man with white hair in a black tuxedo sprint towards the same door. She watched, her heart thudding in her chest, hoping he'd be able to open it, giving them all easy access to leave. But when he reached the door, he stopped and wrestled with the handle. *Locked. Shit.*

An arrow came out of nowhere, shooting from somewhere high up in the room to lodge itself into the man's back. Laina's hand flew to her mouth as another arrow suddenly caught the man in the back of the neck, sending him to the ground. Laina held back the scream as she looked to where the man had fallen. He wasn't alone. More bodies. There were...so many more bodies. Had they all died trying to open the door?

"Fucking Zane," Ryon said, glancing up and to the opposite side of the room. *Zane?* And then he moved.

"What are you—" Laina didn't finish the question. Instead, her heart launched itself into her throat and lodged there as she watched Ryon approach the door. He leaned back and thrust a foot into the panel, sending it bursting open and slamming into the wall behind it. He glanced back and met her gaze. "*Go.*"

Laina hesitated for only a second. She took Max's hand and pulled him with her as they ran. They raced over bodies, past Ryon and through the doorway as he held open the door. Laina stopped just inside the threshold, panting, she glanced around. On one side, some stairs led to the stage and on the other, a long hallway with a green 'exit' sign. *We made it. We made it.* Hope exploded in her chest as she prepared to lead Max and Ryon to the exit door, but then she turned around.

Ryon remained standing *inside* the doorway, bracing himself with one hand on either side of the frame, blocking it. Suddenly, his body jolted forward from some impact that she couldn't see. His eyes turned the colour of molten lava as he gritted his teeth in pain, but still, he continued to block the doorway. Laina let out a cry and started forward—but Max caught her, holding her back.

"Get her out of here," Ryon snarled at Max as his body convulsed with another impact. And another one. And another. Ryon's gaze found Laina's and held there as if, in doing so, he was drawing strength from her. And *God,* how she'd give it if she could.

She watched in horror as Ryon leaned forward and took hold the door handle—and that was when she saw it—the four long arrows with red feathers on the end that protruded from his back. For a split-second, Ryon's gaze met hers, and despite the strain and hardness in his features, his eyes softened with a feeling of sorrow that she felt deep in her chest.

And then he yanked the door closed.

CHAPTER TWENTY-THREE

"Let me help you with that."

Ryon tensed as he heard the King's voice just before the sound of footsteps closed in. He started to turn around, his back screaming in agony, but the King was there. He appeared directly behind Ryon and wrapped a hand around his throat, causing the arrows to dig further into Ryon's flesh. His sword was still sheathed and digging into his back just as much as the arrows on either side of it was. Ryon let out a strangled sound as the King moved closer...and closer. Close enough that Ryon could feel the King's breath on his ear. "Did you think I wouldn't notice you sneaking those pitiful humans out of this room?" The King hissed. "You're weak. Just like I knew you'd be." He punctuated the last word by snapping off one of the arrows.

Unimaginable pain made Ryon cry out, but he couldn't move. He couldn't pull away. The King held his throat firmly and held his body in place by the second arrow. And then he snapped that one too. The King made quick work of snapping the next two arrow ends before stepping back and letting him fall to the floor in a heap. Ryon was left panting, his body vibrating with an intense agony that made his vision waver.

"Times up, gentle males!" the King called out, now from some distance away.

For a fleeting moment, he wondered where Fynn and the others were. He wondered where Kove was. And he wondered if that *fucker* Max had already managed to get Laina out of the building. But just in case, he'd buy them more time.

"You're a coward," Ryon said, knowing the King would be able to hear him clearly over the noise.

"I'm sorry?" The King retorted, incredulously.

Ryon grunted as he used the wall to lift himself up. Pain shot through his back and chest and rippled out like waves of fire throughout his body, but he stood. Swaying, Ryon turned around to face the King. "You're a coward."

One moment Ryon was doing his best to stay on his feet. The next, his back erupted into excruciating pain as it hit the wall, digging those arrows in further. The King had pinned him up against the wall by the throat, and his feet no longer touched the ground. Ryon's hands flew to the King's arm, gripping it tightly as he struggled to gain purchase.

"Would you like to try that again, *boy*?"

Ryon gritted his teeth against the pain and met the King's gaze. "You're..." he let out a cough and tried again, "...a fucking *coward*." He pulled Ryon back and slammed him into the wall. Ryon was barely able to hold back the cry of pain, but he wouldn't give the King the satisfaction of knowing he'd hurt him.

"Once more?" The King seethed, his eyes burning with rage. "I don't think I heard you."

The bubble of laughter exploded from Ryon's mouth.

The King's eyes flared in response, and he loosened his hold on Ryon's throat. Ryon took the opportunity. "You heard me." Another cough. "You want to hide behind the Reds and the Shadows while you use your position to justify the killing of innocent humans. And it's all just to stroke your own ego."

The King peeled back his lips, exposing twin sharp fangs before he slammed Ryon back into the wall so hard that not only did the arrows embed themselves further into his skin, but the plaster on the wall around him cracked under the weight. This time Ryon couldn't help but let out a cry as his body shook with the incomprehensible agony that shot through him. The King released his hold, and Ryon crumpled to the floor.

"Take him to the palace! I want him locked up in the dungeon!" the King called out. Ryon glanced up, his vision blurry from the pain, to see two Reds walking towards him. Ryon closed his eyes. He needed to get the hell out of here. He needed to fade away and shut down any vampiric bonds just in case the King told the Shadows to follow him. He clenched his teeth as he tried to fade, but his body was thrumming with so much pain that it was damn near impossible to focus.

Come on. Come on. Ryon inhaled deeply and tried to concentrate. And just before his body cooperated, and he managed to fade, the two Reds reached out for him—

Only to wrap their hands around nothing.

CHAPTER TWENTY-FOUR

Laina's ears were still ringing from the onslaught of screams over the last hour. Her body trembled as her adrenalin began to dissipate, but as she glanced over at a resting Max on her lounge, she felt nothing but relief—well, relief *and* fear for Ryon, but she couldn't think about that right now. She'd allowed Max to take her out of the Ladwick Community Hall. Together, they bolted to the carpark where they found Max's car and sped to Laina's apartment where they locked the door and collapsed inside. Laina sat against the wall, her knees bent, and her elbows resting on her knees. She did not miss that this was the same position she'd sat in last night after Ryon had saved her from Kove.

The sound of sirens had Laina glancing to the patio door in the distance. The curtains were still drawn, and she had no idea of the time, but it would have to be the middle of the night. Was Brynn in one of those police cars?

"That man..." Max started, his eyes opening as he glanced up to the ceiling. "The one who helped us escape back there, he's the one who found your phone, isn't he?"

"Yes, he is," Laina replied.

Max turned his head to face her, his grey eyes meeting hers. "He's a vampire, isn't he?"

"Yes, he is," she repeated.

"You don't seem surprised by that."

Laina wondered for a moment what to say. She opened her mouth to reply when she heard what sounded like a groan come from the patio.

"What was that?" Max asked, pushing himself up to stand. The sound came again, and Max moved closer to the patio as Laina stood.

"Stay back," Max said as he stepped forward to pull back the curtains slightly and look outside. But Laina stepped forward anyway. She squinted through the darkness as a figure came into view. A tall figure with broad shoulders was leaning heavily on the handrail of her apartment patio.

"Ryon," she said on a breath as relief poured into her. She moved to unlock the sliding door, but Max stepped forward to block her way.

"Don't let him in, Laina."

"What are you doing?" she demanded. "He saved our lives!"

"That doesn't change the fact that he's a vampire! Did you hear the way he threatened me in that hall?"

Laina scoffed. "He's hurt, Max. I need to help him."

When Max just stood there glaring, she pushed past him and opened the sliding door. Ryon was still hunched over the railing, but at least no arrows protruded from his back. When she stepped onto the patio, Ryon pushed himself to stand, and she couldn't help but notice the way his body swayed on his feet. He'd told her he could heal, but he didn't appear to be healing at all. His skin was paler than before, and when she glanced up into those golden eyes of his, the colour seemed a dull comparison to what it had been in the hall.

"You're alive," she whispered.

"That's debatable," Ryon said with a strained chuckle. Laina couldn't hold back the smile that graced her lips. He was okay.

"Come inside," she said.

Ryon's gaze darted to Max briefly. "Am I welcome?"

"No. He is *not* welcome!" Max called out from inside the door. "I've seen enough TV shows to know that he can't come in here without an invite!"

Despite the pain he must have been in, Ryon's lips curled up in amusement at Max's words. And to prove Max wrong, Ryon casually strode—albeit limping slightly—inside Laina's apartment. She followed him inside, fighting back the smile at Max's shocked expression. But then, under the living room light, she noticed the four small round arrow shafts jutting from his back. *Oh, God.* When she didn't see the long arrows protruding from his back, she assumed he—or rather, someone else—had removed them, but now her eyes widened with the realisation. They had been snapped off, and the ends were still wedged into his back.

"Ryon, your...your back," she said softly as Ryon turned to face her and sunk back on the armrest of the lounge. How was he still standing?

Clearly not caring about Ryon's back, Max said, "dammit, Laina, he's a vampire." He glanced at Ryon, "No offence."

Ryon snorted. "None taken."

Laina swung around, pent-up emotions now surging forward. Brynn was constantly trying to tell her what to do and now Max was doing the same. Ryon had saved their lives —and he'd saved hers more times than she could count. She owed him. Hell, *Max* owed him.

"I know he's a vampire, Max." She swallowed down the knot in her throat and finally admitted what she'd been feeling. "But...but I care about him." She heard Ryon shuffle on the armrest of the lounge, but she kept her gaze firmly on Max. When his brows drew together, she lifted her chin and kept going. "I'm going to help him, not just because it's the right thing to do but because I want to. And if you can't accept that, then...then you need to leave."

Max blinked at her for long moments, but his frown remained planted on his face. After what felt like forever, he shook his head and stepped forward. "This is insane. You can't do this, Laina."

Laina waited for the guilt and shame to creep in at Max's words...but it didn't come. She *didn't* feel guilty or ashamed for helping Ryon. If her parents had taught her anything in the short time they'd been in her life, it was to always help someone that needed it. And Ryon needed it.

"She asked you to *leave*," Ryon stated in a threatening voice. Then, as if to drive his point home, he stepped forward, coming up to stand beside Laina.

Max's eyes widened briefly before he looked from Ryon to Laina and back again before he narrowed his gaze on her. "I expected better of you. Think of your parents."

Laina's breath left her in a rush at Max's words. Despite what her parents would think right now, Max's words cut deep. She opened her mouth to say something, but Ryon's voice echoed around the room.

"*Leave!*" he snarled.

Max's eyes widened and not from surprise—he looked terrified. He gave Laina one last glare before he turned for the door and disappeared. And it wasn't until he left that Laina let out the breath she didn't even realise she'd been holding.

CHAPTER TWENTY-FIVE

"I s he your b-boyfriend?" Ryon asked, his voice cracking from the pain. He'd been ten seconds away from picking up that pathetic human man and tossing him out of Laina's apartment. Ryon hoped Max wasn't Laina's boyfriend—and not just because he wanted her for himself. Max had shown no respect for Laina—not after the alley when Ryon had given Laina back her phone and not tonight either. Yes, Max had *attempted* to protect her to some extent, but he'd undermined her and offended her, too. And Laina deserved better than that.

Laina swung around from where she'd been watching the door. It seemed to take her a moment to register Ryon's words before her eyebrows dropped and she shook her head. "What? No." She shook it again. "He was...he *was* my best friend. Although now..." she glanced to the door, a look of sorrow across her face that made Ryon want to fade over there and take her into his arms. "Now I'm not so sure."

Ryon's relief was short lived when Laina suddenly turned to him, her eyes narrowed in confusion. "Wait. Did you think

I would have done…" her voice drifted off as she gestured to the lounge. "Did you think I would have done all of that with you if I had a *boyfriend*?"

"I…" Ryon started, his breath catching as a fresh wave of pain ran through him. "I-I would have taken whatever you were willing to offer." He tried to shrug but the agonising tugging sensation in his back made him wince instead.

"Shit! Ryon, your back!" Laina said, rushing over to him as he arched his back with the pain. "I thought you could heal?"

Ryon shook his head. "I can't while the arrows are still in there. I need to go and find Fy—" he stopped short, realising Laina didn't know who he was talking about. "I need to go find someone who can help me pull them out."

"I'll do it," she said quickly.

He held her gaze for a moment. Even after what happened on the lounge last night, she was willing to help him? He shook his head once more and pushed himself up to stand with a grunt. "I wouldn't do that to you. It's…it's not safe for you to be around me right now." He took a few steps forward and laid a hand on the wall. If he could just get to the patio, he could fade…he didn't know exactly where he would go but maybe one of the Shadows had headed back to the manor. *If* he could fade in his current position.

"Let me help you," Laina persisted, moving to step in front of him.

Ryon desperately wanted to stay. He wanted to spend all day here in her apartment with her, but between the pain and his dire need for blood right now, he didn't trust himself. "You can't help me," he said. "Not with this."

She frowned and placed her hands on her hips, and damn

if she wasn't even more adorable when she was mad. "Why not?"

He shook his head and pushed off the wall, stepping around her. "Just, no."

"Why won't you let me help you? I can take the arrows out."

Thanks to the intense throbbing pain in his back, Ryon's patience was wearing thin. He turned around and limped the two steps to her. "I need more than just these arrows out. That's *why*."

"What..." He knew the moment she understood what he was saying when her eyebrows lifted, and her eyes widened.

"Yeah, didn't think so," he said, hating that he'd been harsh with her. Hating that he'd needed to. He turned and made for the patio, but he heard her voice just as he stepped outside.

"I...I'll feed you," she said hesitantly.

"No," Ryon said, swinging back to face her. The sudden movement sent pain ricocheting through his body, and he doubled over.

Laina was there, her arms at his shoulders. "Ryon? Ryon, are you okay?"

He caught that intoxicating mix of vanilla and cinnamon with a hint of rose, and when he glanced up at her, his fangs lengthened with the need to feed. She gasped and stepped back, eliciting a curse from him as he struggled to pull himself to stand. "I don't want to hurt you," he said, panting. "But I need to feed, and I won't be able to control myself if I stay here."

Laina watched him for a moment before she stepped closer. "I trust you. Feed from me." Ryon began to shake his head again, but Laina stepped forward and placed a hand on his chest. "Please."

Despite the agonising pain, a shiver of excitement rippled through Ryon at the thought of taking her vein. He didn't trust his voice to work, so he swallowed hard and tried, anyway. "We...We need to get these arrows out first."

Laina nodded her understanding. "Can you walk to the bathroom?"

Ryon let Laina guide him to the bathroom. The room itself was simple, with a bath and shower, basin, and toilet, but there was no mistaking it to be a human woman's bathroom. The number of colourful bottles around the place gave it away. Her scent was more prominent in here and he fought back the urge to take her blood even with those damn arrows in his back.

Standing in the middle of the bathroom, Ryon kept his back to Laina as he bit through the pain and shrugged out of his leather jacket. The four holes in the leather were stained with blood and sat symmetrically opposite each other, perfectly placed so that it avoided that sword—thanks to Zane's aiming. Ryon unsheathed the sword and threw it on the floor, then draped his jacket over the towel rack beside the shower and reached for the hem of his shirt. He let out a strangled sound as he lifted his shirt over his head, ignoring the intense tugging sensation as the skin pulled taut around the arrow heads. Seeing the slit at the front of his shirt sent a rush of anger and disappointment through him. He couldn't believe Kove was going to kill Laina. *I'm going to fucking kill Zane. And then I'll kill Kove.* Glancing down, he took in the slow-healing red, angry wound covered in dried blood caused by Kove's sword. An inch higher, and it would have gone through his heart. He stepped up to the basin, leaning his outstretched arms on its edge as Laina moved into his reflection from the mirror before him. She stood at his back, her eyes drifting over the wounds.

Ryon's gaze roamed over her face, her neck and the deep V of the dress that exposed the skin between her breasts. "You..." his voice cracked as the need to be with her surged through him, dulling the pain for a mere moment. Her eyes flicked up to meet his in the reflection, and he tried again, "you look...*spectacular* in that dress."

She gave a small smile as her cheeks pinkened with a blush that made him want to turn around and press a kiss there. But he'd done enough damage. Instead, he glanced down, tightening his hold on the basin edge. "You don't have to do this," Ryon said quietly.

"I want to," she replied, her gaze dropping to his back once more. "Who did this to you?"

He gritted his teeth when he felt her hand on one of the short pieces of the arrow that protruded from his back. "The King." Gripping the basin tightly—careful not to break it—he braced himself as Laina yanked out the remnant of one arrow. Pain exploded in his body, and he fell forward, placing an outstretched hand on the mirror above.

"The King?" she asked, slightly out of breath. "Is he the one who set those rules you've mentioned?" Was she trying to distract him by talking? If she was...he was grateful for it.

"Yeah," Ryon replied. "But he has since revoked them. There are no more rules anymore." *Yank.* Ryon couldn't hold back the curse that exploded from his mouth as Laina pulled out the second arrow, and he heard a clang as they were both thrown into a nearby bin. *Two more to go.*

He glanced up into the reflection as a bead of sweat trickled down his forehead. His arms trembled from restraining himself—both from the need for blood and from the pain—but when her green eyes met his, he felt as though she were giving him the strength he needed to go on. Her gaze was apologetic, but her chin was lifted as if no matter what she was feeling or thinking, she would do whatever it took to get the arrows out. This little human woman was blowing his mind. He was awed at how someone so petite and vulnerable could be so strong and so brave.

"Those rules...they were the only thing keeping vampires from killing humans, weren't they?"

Ryon nodded. Her gaze drifted to his back again, and she placed a hand on his shoulder to guide him down over the basin. *Yank.* Ryon grunted as she pulled the third arrow out. "Is that what this is? Are the arrows punishment for letting Max and I go free?"

Ryon shook his head. "No, it was a warning."

Laina's eyes widened and met his again in the mirror before she asked, "what is the King planning to do? I mean, are we safe here?"

He readjusted his position on the basin. "We're safe for tonight." *Yank.* Ryon groaned and hunched forward. *They're out.* His back was already feeling the reprieve, but the wounds would remain open until he could heal. And he couldn't heal until he fed.

Laina's eyes shot to his in the reflection. "What do you mean, for tonight?"

Ryon took a moment to catch his breath before he turned around. "The King won't do anything else tonight." *I hope.*

He leaned back against the basin and ran his eyes over

Laina. That dress accentuated every curve of her body. His eyes devoured her, and he felt himself grow hard as a result. Laina's breath seemed to quicken, and his gaze darted to see that pink flush across her cheeks again. Had she caught him looking at her?

Laina stepped back and sat down on the side of the bath, resting her elbows on her knees, and that was when he saw the blood. Her fingertips were covered in blood, *his* blood. "Here, let me..." he started. He turned around and found a folded face cloth nearby. He ran it under water for a few seconds then made his way over to her. She frowned, but those beautiful features of hers softened when she saw what he was about to do. He knelt, wincing at the still open wounds at his back, and took one of her hands in his. Then he began to wipe away the remnants of blood with the cloth.

Her hands were so warm, so soft, and as he continued to wipe her skin clean, he couldn't help but look at his own skin. He hated the way his marred flesh was such a contrast to her flawless one. Although, it was quite the metaphor, wasn't it? The scarred vampire and the stunning human. The monster and the goddess. The beast and the beauty. The dark and the light.

When her hands were as clean as they could get with merely a face cloth, he stayed where he was. They both did. "I'm sorry I dragged you into my world," he said suddenly. Her green gaze lifted to meet his.

Laina's eyes held his for long moments before she lifted her hand from his grasp and placed it on his chest, right over the barely healed wound from Kove's sword. "I'm not," she said. "I'm not sorry."

Ryon couldn't help but notice the way Laina's throat

moved as she swallowed hard, as she pulled her hand away from his chest, making him instantly miss the touch. She suddenly looked nervous as she glanced down to her fidgeting hands at her lap. He frowned, not understanding why.

He opened his mouth to ask when she glanced up. "I'm ready for you to drink from me now."

CHAPTER TWENTY-SIX

What the hell was Laina doing? Would she really let a vampire drink from her? Ryon was looking at her with a mix of apprehension and desperation. He needed to heal—that was a fact. And he could only do that if he fed— also a fact. And the only one with the ability to offer that right now? *Her*—Another fact. She swallowed the knot in her throat as nervousness sunk into her gut. Would he drink too much? Would he drain her completely? Would she die tonight...like her parents had?

Ryon cupped her cheeks, and, as if reading her thoughts, he said, "I'll only take the bare minimum. And I won't hurt you. I'll...I'll try not to. If you want me to stop—at any time, just say the words, okay?" *God,* she felt so weak. So *vulnerable* right now. And she hated it. Again, as if he'd read her thoughts, he said, "you have the power here, okay? I'll stop as soon as you say so."

She lifted her chin and nodded. He pulled away from her and placed the facecloth that he'd so carefully cleaned her hands with into the basin before turning back around. Then, for the first time since he'd taken off his shirt, she allowed her eyes to wander. Kove's stab wound remained red and angry and covered with dried blood, but at least it wasn't still bleeding. His shoulders were broad and muscular, and as she perused his chest and the ripples of corded muscle at his stomach, she noticed a dark, fine dusting of hair that led from his naval down to the waistband of his jeans.

"Don't do that." Laina's head snapped back up. Ryon's eyes were slightly brighter than before. Still, as he stood there with his legs splayed and his powerful body on display, she couldn't deny that deep down, she wasn't entirely against him feeding from her. A part of her wanted to know what it felt like. Those lashes of his swept down, hooding his eyes, but not enough to hide the intensity in his stare. "Don't look at me like you did last night on that lounge." *Oh. That.* Her eyes darted through the open bathroom door to the lounge where they'd kissed, touched...and were minutes away from bringing each other to release. And then it dawned on her. *A bit of give and take.*

"But isn't that what you do? Give pleasure to take blood?" She knew she had no right to ask him this, but it had been bothering her since the night in the Ladwick Hotel.

He fell to his knees before her and took her hands. "Not with you. *Never* with you." She sucked in a breath at the raw honesty in his tone and in his eyes. "I won't deny that I don't want to taste your blood—it's been on my mind since the first night I saw you in that alley—but I'd never treat you as those humans I've fed from. It was a necessity, and when I...gave back, it was because I didn't like feeling as though I were using these innocent humans for my own needs. But you...you're different. You're so much more

170

important than that. You're so much more important to *me*."

He reached forward and tucked a strand of hair behind her ear. "I've been living off blood bags, Laina. I haven't taken a vein since the night I met you in that alley. I've wanted to, I've *needed* to, but...no one's scent..." he shook his head again. "No one comes close to you. It would be like going out with a craving for a steak dinner, but the only thing on the menu was lentils."

She chuckled at that. Ryon cupped her cheek and smiled that heart-stopping smile, sending ripples of warmth through her. "Laina, I want you. Only you. I won't deny that I want your blood, your body, and your heart, but I'm not about to take anything that you're not willing to give."

Laina's heart thudded in her chest, making her feel like it would explode at any moment. Ryon's words had struck her very soul...and she believed every one of them.

She inhaled deeply and sat up straighter as Ryon pulled his hand away. *Now or never.* She reached up and pulled her hair to one side, exposing her throat. Ryon's gaze riveted to her neck, his eyes flaring a golden colour. Ryon's features hardened, his lips pulled back slightly, and his fangs lengthened before her very eyes. He looked hungry—no, he looked *famished*.

She squeezed her eyes closed, her breaths growing ragged as she tilted her head and waited to feel the sting of the bite. Would it hurt much? Her question was answered when she felt the featherlight touch of Ryon's mouth at her neck. She parted her lips on a gasp, expecting pain at any moment. But no pain came. Instead, she felt Ryon's soft lips just under her ear, eliciting a moan from her. Suddenly, any apprehension she felt withered away when his tongue ran down the length of her neck and then planted an open-mouthed kiss at her collarbone, sending ripples of heat through her body before he moved across to her shoulder.

She flung open her eyes when he pulled back. She wanted to ask what he was doing, but all thoughts vanished when he lifted her arm and leaned down to kiss the inside of her elbow. Those golden eyes stared back at her with an intensity that sent her heart rate into a spin and her body vibrating with desire. Butterflies exploded in her stomach as he moved down the inside of her arm to her wrist, his eyes never leaving hers as his mouth closed over the pale skin there.

Laina's breath hitched as a slight sting ricocheted from her wrist up her arm but then disappeared, leaving her only with the surprisingly erotic sensation of Ryon tugging at her wrist with each swallow. Hearing a soft groan, she lifted her gaze from his mouth to see his eyes now blazing a bright gold as they stared back at her from under heavy lids.

Ryon's hand found her thigh, giving it a small squeeze, the action sending ripples of arousal through her body and straight to her core. She closed her eyes at the intensity of the need running through them—between them. Without realising what she was doing, she lifted her free hand and ran it through his hair. He moaned in response, and after what felt like too short a time, he released her wrist and she found herself immediately missing the feel of him there. She opened her eyes to see his tongue flick out over the two puncture wounds, and to her disbelief, they healed before her very eyes.

He pulled away and stood up, breathing hard. He was clearly as affected by her as she was with him. But she wasn't done. Unfiltered arousal and frantic desire coursed through her, making her want to finish what they'd started yesterday. Despite Ryon accidentally nipping her last night, she knew he wouldn't hurt her—he'd proven that time and time again. And maybe it was lust, maybe it was an effect of the feeding, or maybe it was the connection between them, but she wanted more. She *needed* more.

Without another thought, Laina stood and looked up at him. "Kiss me," she said roughly.

Ryon's eyes searched her face for a moment before they grew heavy-lidded and dropped to her lips. His big chest was rising and falling, and with the wild look in his eyes and his tussled hair, he looked as though he were on the verge of losing control. And he'd never looked sexier.

"Kiss me," she urged, those fiery eyes meeting hers once more.

And then he kissed her. She moaned, closing her eyes when he pressed his lips against hers, his hands flying to her hips and gripping them tightly. He yanked her to him, roughly, *possessively*—and she loved it. She could feel his own arousal, hard and hot against her stomach and when she pressed her body closer to his, it was his moan that echoed around the room this time.

One of Ryon's hands released her hip to come up and cradle the back of her head, allowing him to deepen the kiss as she opened her mouth to him. His tongue darted inside, and she mewled at the contact. And then she was moving. Ryon had moved unbelievably fast, closing the bathroom door, and pushing her back against it, his hand absorbing the shock of the impact behind her head. He released her mouth and moved down, kissing, and sucking at her chin, then her neck before making his way down between her breasts. Laina's breaths came in pants as Ryon pulled back, and she opened her eyes to see his gaze riveted to the plunging neckline.

"I fucking *love* this dress," he said in a low rumble as he ran a fingertip over her collarbone and down the exposed skin between her breasts. When he reached the base of the V, he followed one side of the neckline up, letting his finger glide just underneath the material and causing her nipples to harden in response. "You're so damn beautiful," he said, his eyes meeting hers. Then, his heated gaze softened. "Dawn's coming. I should go."

The breath caught in Laina's throat, and she felt as though she'd just been dropped into a bathtub of freezing cold water. "I don't want you to go."

Ryon smiled and tucked a strand of hair behind her ear. "I don't want to go either, but if I don't leave now, I'll have to stay until nightfall."

"So, stay," she breathed.

His lips parted on a breath, and after a long moment, he said, "if I stay here, I can't promise I'll keep my hands to myself."

"So, don't."

Laina squealed when Ryon abruptly threw her over his shoulder, and she had to hold that plunging neckline of hers closed. Despite everything that had happened tonight, Laina found herself laughing—*actually* laughing—as he opened the bathroom door and found his way to her bedroom before throwing her on the bed. Her laughter died down as Ryon walked over to the window and closed the blinds before turning on her bedside lamp. His heated gaze never left her body as he swiftly took off his shoes and climbed onto the bed. Laina's gaze landed on the stab wound on his chest. It was nothing but a pink scar now, and she absentmindedly lifted her wrist to see the puncture wounds were completely gone. "You really can heal," she said.

"Because of you. Because of your blood," Ryon said as he moved to straddle her hips.

She sucked in a breath when his fingertips went back to tracing the V of the neckline of her dress. Laina's gaze roamed over him, over the rippling muscles of his chest, his lean stomach and followed that light dusting of dark hair down to the waistband of his black jeans. The large, thick bulge that caught her eye there made her stomach clench with need, her mouth salivating at the thought of what was behind the cloth.

"Have I mentioned that I love this dress?" Ryon asked as his gaze flicked to hers. "Easy access."

Before she could respond, Ryon pulled the neckline of her dress across, exposing one of her breasts to the cool air before covering it with his hand. Laina let out a mewl and reached out to grip his hair as he leaned down to take her aching nipple in his mouth. She writhed underneath him as he shoved the material of the dress aside and reached for her other breast. He released her and lifted his head, those golden eyes blazing as they looked back at her with a need that matched her own.

"One day, if you want me to, I'm going to feed from you here..." he let the words linger as he ran his fingertips over her nipple. Laina's breaths were ragged as he reached down to her thigh, fisting the material of her dress, and pulling it up until she could feel his skin against hers. "And here..." he said, giving her thigh a squeeze. She bit her lip as Ryon's fingers trailed across to her core before he glanced up at her. "And here..." he said, never taking his gaze from hers as he moved her underwear aside and ran a finger between her already slick folds.

Laina moaned loudly, needing more of him. His gaze dropped to where his finger was exploring her. "*Fuck,* I want to taste you." He glanced back up at her. "But for tonight, I just want to be inside you." His finger explored the sensitive area just outside her entrance. "May I?"

She nodded and closed her eyes, her body writhing, moving—*searching*—for him. He delved a finger inside her, making her moan louder. But it wasn't enough. She wanted more. She *needed* more. "More?" he asked. Had she spoken out loud?

"Yes," she breathed out and watched as he removed his finger and lifted it to his mouth, sucking it. *Oh.* He leaned up on his knees and started to undo the button of his jeans. Her fingers itched to touch him. His physique, the way his body moved, the way his body healed...she was in awe of everything about him.

Reaching forward, she placed a hand on his chest, right above the healing stab wound and the dried blood that surrounded it. Ryon closed his eyes as she ran a hand over the hard ridges of his abs and down, over that dark trail of hair until she reached his waistband. He'd undone the button, but Laina took care of his zipper, biting her lip when her finger brushed over his hard length. *Commando.*

Ryon let out a groan and opened his eyes. He caught her hand, guiding it further inside his pants until she could —*barely*—wrap her hand around him. She stroked him once... twice...and then he pulled her hand away with a curse. "You're going to make me..." he shook his head, and she watched his Adam's apple bob as he shoved his pants down, taking them off completely and freeing a painfully hard erection. She gasped at the sheer size of him, but when he tore off her underwear and lay over her to grind his hard length against her pelvis, she wanted nothing more than to have him inside of her, stretching her.

"Ryon," she gasped, looking up into those intense golden coloured eyes. "I need you."

He closed his eyes. "Say it again," he growled with another thrust against her pelvis. She moaned louder, feeling his hardness just above her core, *just* above where she needed him to be.

"I need you!" she almost yelled, reaching up to grip his hair.

He opened his eyes and looked down at her as she released his hair to cup his face. His expression blew her away. He looked at her as if the stars and the moon in his world began and ended with her. And then he kissed her—hard—as he slipped inside her. She gasped into his mouth, releasing his face to grip the bedsheets as the sensation of being filled by him ignited a fire deep inside her, sending ripples of ecstasy through her body. It felt so *damn* good.

Then he moved. He pulled back before thrusting forward again...and again, finding a rhythm that was slow at first and then building, sending her into a frenzied crescendo of unbearable pleasure. She was panting through her moans as she lifted her hands to his strong back, to feel the muscle and sinew flexing with each thrust. His fangs lengthened, and for a split-second, she thought he might bite her again but instead, he leaned forward and kissed her as his hand drifted down to stroke her core.

Pleasure exploded through her, a blazing trail of fire ricocheting around her body and sending her crashing over the precipice. He pulled back from the kiss just as she closed her eyes and cried out his name, digging her nails into his back as she found her release. When she opened them again, she saw Ryon's powerful body strained with tension before he threw his head back on a curse. He stilled as the corded muscles in his neck pulled taut, and she felt his length pulse inside of her, exploding with his own release. After long moments, he glanced down, meeting her eyes with satisfaction and...tenderness.

She reached up, cupping the back of his head and pulled him down for another kiss. This time it wasn't hard or desperate. It was soft and languid. He deepened the kiss as his fangs gently grazed her lips, their tongues entwining just as much as their bodies. When he finally pulled back, his eyes roamed over every inch of her face, and at that moment, time stood still. The world faded away. There was no death, no war, no vampires, no humans—nothing but them. Laina and Ryon.

CHAPTER TWENTY-SEVEN

Ryon awoke to the sound of buzzing as Laina's scent of vanilla mixed with cinnamon and rose surrounded him, reminding him of everything that happened before he fell asleep. The room was dark, but he couldn't tell if that was thanks to it being close to sundown or the pulled shutters. Still, through the darkness, he was able to look around her room. It was simple with plain white walls, no pictures or posters and every other piece of furniture in the room was a pale timber colour with black accents. There was a large plant in one corner of the room and a few smaller pot plants on the dresser, but besides that, only a few personal items sat on top of surfaces. It was modern, minimalistic, and very Laina. Only she could turn 'simple' into something stylish.

A smile graced his lips as he thought about last night. About the way she looked in that dress, the way her body felt underneath his, and the way she'd called out his name with her release. And then there was her blood. He hadn't expected her to offer to feed him, but when he took her vein...the taste of her blood was better than anything he'd ever tasted. *Sweeter* than anything he'd ever tasted. When she exposed her neck, giving him easy access, he'd almost gone crazy with need—but then her breath had hitched and he sensed her apprehension, so he decided to take her wrist instead. He didn't want her to think she was just there to be used like all those other humans he'd fed from. He wanted to respect her body and earn her trust.

The buzzing echoed around the room again, and this time he recognised it as his phone. It must have fallen out of the back pocket of his jeans when he'd taken them off last night. Laina was still sound asleep with her back against his chest and his arm over her waist. He peeled himself away from Laina to roll over to where the buzz of his phone was coming from. His gaze searched the wooden floorboards. *There.* He spotted his phone just under the bed and, careful not to wake Laina, he leaned over and plucked it from the floor.

Unlocking it, he noticed the time in the top corner of the screen. *Almost sundown.* He'd missed three texts from Fynn, but he scrolled past the first two to open the last one:

Ry, where are you?

The King is looking for you. He's sent every damn Red out there to search for you.

I hope you've found a good fucking hiding spot.

Ryon frowned and read over the text another three times. He expected the King to be furious that one of his enforcers went rogue, but not to care enough to send out a search party. And in fact, Ryon wasn't the one to go rogue—the King was. When the King revoked the very rules that kept the vampires in Ladwick safe and away from human eyes, he turned his back on his own kind. Instead, he signed them up for a fate filled with war, fear, and ultimate death.

Laina stirred beside him, and he set aside his phone, leaning over to gently kiss her shoulder. "Shower with me?" Ryon whispered against her ear. He could feel the dried blood on his chest and back, and he knew Laina would likely be desperate to get out of the dress she'd worn last night—and fallen asleep in.

She smiled and snuggled closer to him but didn't open her eyes. "Not yet. It's too early."

He chuckled softly. "I think you'll find it's late. We slept all day."

Laina's eyes flung open. "What?"

He couldn't wipe the smile off his face as he laid back and watched her jump out of bed, her formal dress now skewed and crinkled. He could get used to waking up to this each night. She rushed to her dresser and began rummaging through drawers and pulling out clothes before she left the room. He chuckled as he followed her into the bathroom, where she had piled her fresh clothes up on the edge of the bathtub and started running the shower. She glanced over her shoulder at him, and he half expected her to tell him to leave... but she didn't. Instead, she held his gaze as she pulled down the thin straps of her dress and let it fall to the ground.

Ryon's chuckle died in his throat as he let out a curse and grew hard in an instant. He palmed his mouth absentmindedly as his eyes ran over the length of her body and back up to land on her backside...her bare backside. *Because I tore off her underwear last night*, he realised. She stepped into the shower and turned around, closing her eyes, and throwing her head back under the water. He watched, mesmerised with the way her breasts swayed with the movement as she began to wash her hair. *Fuck.* His fingers twitched beside him—he itched to touch her. Her eyes opened, and she smiled at him. "I thought we were showering together?"

He shook his head with a smirk, almost tearing his clothes apart to join her under the water. It was a small shower, but he wasn't complaining. Instead, he made the most of the confined space by standing so close behind her that his already painfully hard erection was up against her backside, then he reached around and cupped her perfect breasts. "Little temptress," he whispered against her ear. "I think I prefer you without the dress."

The sudden and deafening sound of an alarm rang out loudly through what sounded like the entire apartment. Ryon went rigid, but Laina turned around in his arms. "It's okay. It's just the fire alarm. Someone's probably just burned their dinner."

He shook his head as a wave of dread ran through him. "I don't think so." He rinsed off briefly and stepped out of the shower as Laina finished washing her hair and lathering her body. He would have accepted ten more arrows in his back to watch her shower herself, but he needed to be alert right now. He barely dried himself off before he pulled on his jeans and the shirt he'd left in here. He put on his leather jacket and sheathed his sword before he tensed, catching the familiar scent of Reds from the cracked bathroom window. He turned to Laina, who was getting out of the shower, just as the alarm sound changed to the deafening evacuation signal. "This isn't just a fire alarm."

"What's going on?" Laina asked as she dried off and dressed in the more practical outfit of jeans and a grey jumper.

He glanced to the window before looking back to Laina. Ryon knew the King was relentless in taking down those who didn't agree with him. Hell, look what he did to Soran. No matter where Ryon went, the King would find a way to track him down. More and more Reds would be sent to find him, and any human—including Laina—that was in the way would be killed. And Ryon couldn't live with himself if something happened to her. His stomach roiled as he realised that there was only one thing to do to keep Laina safe.

Ryon leaned forward and cupped Laina's cheek with his free hand. "It's the King. He's here for me. I don't want to leave you, but I need you to be safe. And you won't be if you're with me. You should be safe enough if you leave now. I need you to get changed and go out into the hall. Follow everyone as they evacuate and blend in as best you can." Laina hesitated before nodding jerkily, her eyes wide with a fear that he wished he could take away. "When they let everyone back into the apartment, I need you to pack your things and leave. Do you hear me?" When she said nothing, he reiterated, "Laina, I need to know that you understand. You have to leave Ladwick. Even just temporarily. Do you hear?"

He didn't wait for her to answer. He leaned in and placed his lips against hers, *hard.* It was desperate. It was goodbye. It was a gallows kiss. A deep-seated sadness crept into his chest at the thought of never seeing Laina again, but he needed to do whatever he could to keep her safe. Even if that meant handing himself over to the King. After a long moment, Ryon reluctantly pulled back from the kiss and, without another word, faded out of the bathroom window.

CHAPTER TWENTY-EIGHT

It took all of five minutes for Laina to finish getting dressed and open the door to her apartment. She didn't take anything with her because...well, she had nothing to take. Last night, Max had opened the door to her apartment with his spare set of keys, but everything else—including her own set of keys, her phone, and wallet—were all in the clutch that she'd left behind in the hall.

Her mind was a mix of chaotic thoughts as she made her way out of her apartment and into the hallway. Her breaths felt heavy, her palms sweaty and her stomach churning with worry as she played out every worst-case scenario in her head. Would Ryon be safe? What was he going to do? What if something happened to him? What they'd shared last night, it had been...*perfect. He* was perfect. They way he'd touched her, the way he'd *filled* her, the way he'd made her feel...it had all felt so *special.* And damn, if her body wasn't feeling slightly achy from the onslaught of pleasure he'd wrung from her—in the best way possible.

Brynn was probably losing her mind over not being able to

contact her all day—and why hadn't Brynn come to her apartment? Had something happened to her? Laina pushed the thoughts away and joined the line of people making their way calmly down the stairs and out to the fire escape. A part of her wanted to scream out and tell them all that this wasn't just another burnt toast fiasco, that a war was coming, and that vampires were real. She wanted to tell them all to leave Ladwick. Just like Ryon has told her to do, which was *never* going to happen because she couldn't just up and leave Brynn, or even Max, despite the jerk he'd been to her last night. But she had chosen to agree with Ryon, anyway. Laina had no idea what he had planned to do, but she didn't want to be a distraction for him.

She made her way out of the building and across the road to the park with the rest of the occupants. The sun had just barely set, but it was dark enough that the streetlamps had flickered on. There was an eery gloom about the night, as if even the trees knew the war was brewing, and she wrapped her arms around herself as a shiver ran down her spine.

"Laina!" She swung around to see an out of breath Brynn in her police uniform pushing her way through the people. "Oh, thank *God* you're alright," her sister said, pulling her into a bone-breaking embrace. It was unusual to get a hug from Brynn, but right now, she'd take it. She closed her eyes and relished in the moment. She threw her own arms around her and held on tightly. All of their arguing and disagreements now felt so trivial in the face of everything that had happened.

Long moments passed before Laina pulled back. "I'm okay...I'm okay. What are you doing here?"

"I just got here," Brynn replied. "I've been trying to call you all day. I worked a double shift and only just got off, so I came straight here." Before Laina could reply, Brynn glanced around at the crowds of people now piling into the park. Then she reached for Laina's arm and guided her to the side, away from the people. "They're *real*, Laina. Vampires are fucking *real*."

Laina pursed her lips, hesitating as Brynn's brown eyes searched her face in confusion. "You're not surprised," Brynn said, taking a step back and frowning. The betrayal was evident on her face and Laina's chest tightened in response.

"I..." Laina considered lying to Brynn but in the end, she figured there was no point. "I found out a few days ago."

Brynn recoiled. "What! And you didn't tell me?" Brynn's voice got louder as she crossed her arms over her chest and glared. "Laina, this changes *everything*. Why didn't you tell me?" Before Laina could respond, Brynn's gaze dropped to the ground. "This means our parents...the rumours were true, they really were..." Her voice trailed off for a moment. When she looked up again, her eyes went wide at something over Laina's shoulder.

Just before Laina could swing around to see what was over her shoulder, a man suddenly appeared behind Brynn. *No, not a man*, she thought as a jolt of fear ran through her when her gaze landed on his red eyes. A *vampire.*

"*Sleep*, humans."

And just like that, the darkness consumed her.

———

Laina came to on some form of hard cushion. She lifted her hand to shield her eyes against the blinding light that came from somewhere above her. She was vaguely aware that she was lying down, and it was cold...so cold. The sound of shouts had her pulling her hand away from her face as she suddenly recalled what had happened. She sat up and looked around. She was in a...*cell*? Carved stone covered the ceiling and three walls—the fourth was a wall-to-wall glass panel with a metallic door in the middle. And on the other side of that glass stood the vampire who had put them to sleep. *Brynn. Where was Brynn?* Ignoring the vampire, she stood and glanced across the room as a wave of panic ran through her. But there, on the other bed in the cell, was a woman lying on her side, facing the wall, wearing a police uniform.

"Laina Hawkins?" the male asked in a deep voice. Brynn began to stir and Laina sagged with relief before swinging around to face the vampire.

Fear surged through her, but tendrils of rage broke through the fear. She'd been *kidnapped*. Brynn had been kidnapped. After everything she'd been through the past few days, she was *done* with being scared. "Fuck you!" she shouted, squeezing her fists so tightly at her sides that she could feel her nails digging into the skin.

He smirked, lifting a brow as he tilted his head in an animalistic way, those red eyes never leaving hers. "Are you Laina Hawkins?" he asked again.

"That's her," another male said as he came into view and stood beside the first. He had short blond hair that was slicked back, and his eyes glowed the same scarlet red colour as the first—but he was dressed differently. Whilst the first man wore black slacks and a black shirt, this man wore blue jeans, a black shirt, and a black leather jacket with ribbed sleeves—the same kind that Ryon wore.

"She's the one Ryon helped escape," the second male said,

repositioning the crossbow that hung over his shoulder. Laina's breath hitched as her gaze drifted between the crossbow to the arrows sheathed at his back with red feathers on the end. Immediately her mind went back to that hall as she had watched Ryon reach for the door—and she had seen the arrows with red feathers that protruded from his back. They were the same arrows. *Fucking Zane,* Ryon had said. *Zane.* Anger quickly turned to rage as she gritted her teeth at what he'd done to Ryon.

She heard the creak of a bed and swung around to see Brynn swinging her legs over the side of the bed to sit up. Brynn rubbed her temple as she looked down at the ground for a moment but then as if recalling what had happened, she snapped her head up to see Laina. The relief was evident on her face, but then Brynn's eyes darted to the males standing outside the glass. Brynn blanched, standing up slowly...ever so slowly. "Zane?"

Laina frowned, confused. She darted a look at Zane—who looked to be smirking even more—before glancing back to Brynn. "Do you...know him?"

Brynn's wide eyes tore from Zane and landed on Laina as she nodded gravely. "He was my boyfriend."

CHAPTER TWENTY-NINE

Ryon didn't have time to make sure Laina made it out with the other humans in the apartment, but there was no reason for her to be in danger. For whatever reason, the King wanted Ryon. And Ryon would oblige, but first, he needed to do something. As he faded onto the front grass area of the Shadows mansion, he bolted up the steps, taking two at a time until he reached the front door. Pushing the heavy door open, he ran down the hallway and through the door that would take him down to the armoury. He trusted his sword and his strength, but tonight, he needed everything he could find.

After strapping a holster under his leather jacket, he sheathed two switchblades and pocketed a third. Then, he made his way down to the kitchen and found a few blood bags that had been left behind. Laina's blood had healed him, had satiated his need for replenishment, but he needed more if he wanted to keep up his strength. He opened the first bag, took a sip, and almost spat out the vile liquid. It tasted like dirt compared to Laina's blood, but he forced himself to finish it, and then the second.

Wiping his mouth on his sleeve, he pulled out his phone and walked back to the main lobby. Fynn had texted him, he'd warned Ryon about the King searching for him. So, he couldn't be on the King's side, right? After all, Fynn had been the first to admit that barging into Ladwick hall to kill those humans had been wrong. Maybe he could reach out to Fynn... He bit the bullet and called Fynn, halting when it went straight to voicemail. Fynn never turned off his phone. Dread seeped into his stomach. Something was wrong. Something was *very* wrong.

He placed his phone in his back pocket and made his way through the dark lobby and back to the entrance doors. He reached for the handle, cracking the door open slightly—

And was met with the overwhelming scent of Reds.

He swiftly closed the door again and stepped back, his fists clenching and unclenching. He didn't see how many Reds were outside, but there were too many for one Shadow to take down. When the King sent those Reds for him in the hall, Ryon ran. When they came for him in Laina's apartment, he ran. But no more. He would stay and fight this time, even if it meant sacrificing his own life to protect those he cared for. To protect Laina.

He unsheathed the sword from his back and yanked open the door with his free hand. Ryon bared his fangs and snarled at the ten or so Reds that stared back at him with scarlet red eyes from the base of the stairs. And then he attacked. He wasn't arrogant enough to think for a second that he alone could beat ten Reds, but with his experience and strength, there was always a chance. A *slim* chance—but a chance, nonetheless. The Red's backed up a few steps and crouched, hissing, and bearing their fangs as he approached with his outstretched sword. Unlike Ryon, the Reds didn't use weapons, and he hoped he could use that to his advantage.

Ryon lunged, thrusting his sword out and catching an unsuspecting Red through the chest. They weren't expecting him to be ready for a fight, but when the male dropped to the ground, the nine remaining Reds hissed and snarled in response. He'd angered them—*Good*. Maybe they'd make a mistake, and Ryon would get that slim chance of survival after all.

The Reds began circling him, and he found himself spinning, unsure which of them he'd rather have at his back. Ryon lunged again, but the Red ducked, with a speed that only a fresh vampire had, as Ryon's sword caught him in the shoulder. Another one gripped Ryon's free arm, yanking him back and moving at incredible speed to lift his arm and bite down on his wrist. Ryon roared and hefted his sword upwards, getting the vampire square in the chest. The male let go of Ryon's arm and stumbled back, but only for another one to step in.

Ryon's sword arm was yanked back, and someone bit into it and released, ripping the skin, and leaving a gaping, bleeding hole in Ryon's wrist—but Ryon couldn't feel it. He couldn't feel anything but burning rage. He yelled as his hand gripped the sword's hilt harder and used the power of his strength to swing it around, slicing through the Red's neck until his head was no longer attached.

Three Reds were down now, but Ryon was far from triumphant as two Reds came from behind and caught his arms. He fought against their holds and against the pain that was now pushing through the numbing adrenaline, but it was no use. They held firm as a third Red came forward and, with the speed of lightning and launched himself at Ryon, tearing into his neck. Ryon snarled as pain erupted from the bite as a fourth Red stepped up to him—

Only to abruptly halt when the tip of a sword appeared at the front of his chest.

The Red's eyes went wide, and he fell forward in a heap. Ryon's shocked gaze followed the male down to the ground and then back up to see...two familiar gold eyes staring back at him.

"Am I late?" Kove asked casually as the two Reds on either side of him released his arms.

Ryon stepped free of the Reds as Kove effortlessly swung his sword at one of the other Reds heading his way. One smooth flick of Kove's wrist and the male's head fell from his body. Ryon's momentary disbelief was thwarted when a hiss from behind reminded him he still had work to do.

"What the *fuck* are you doing here?" Ryon gritted out as he caught a Red in the stomach. The strength in his arms waned from the injuries, but he clenched his teeth together and tried again, catching the Red through the heart.

"Helping you, you ungrateful bastard," Kove replied through his grunts as he took care of another one.

"*Ungrateful*?" Ryon spat incredulously. He swung his sword with both hands as another Red came at him and Ryon swiftly took off his head. "You...*stabbed* me!"

Kove snarled, and Ryon heard the thud of a body hit the ground. "About that. I...I'm sorry."

Ryon stopped mid-fight to look over at Kove. He had never apologised for anything, and it...sounded genuine. Ryon glanced back just as the Red launched himself at Ryon, knocking him to the ground. The air left his lungs on impact, but he didn't waste a second before he thrust the sword into the vampire's chest, not waiting to check that he was dead before throwing him off and pushing up to stand. "You damn near killed me," Ryon growled. "You *could* have killed Laina!"

Kove's eyes darted away from Ryon as if he was too ashamed to make eye contact. "I'm a lot older than you, Ryon." Ryon narrowed his eyes, wondering what that had to do with anything. None of the Shadows knew exactly how old Kove was, but how was that relevant? "I've seen what humans are capable of." Kove sighed and made his way over to where one of the Reds lay motionless, before he knelt and used the male's shirt to clean the blood off his blade.

Keeping his gaze lowered, Kove said, "I've lost someone I cared for. Someone I...I *loved*...because of them." He shook his head. "I didn't think humans could bring any good into our world." Kove's now brown eyes flicked up to meet Ryon's. "Last night, I *did* want to kill Laina."

Ryon gripped his sword hilt tightly as a snarl tore from his throat. Kove shook his head and ducked his gaze again. "I wanted to save you from being hurt like I was. But then you pushed Laina out of the way and took her place at the end of that blade..." Kove's voice trailed off, and Ryon found his grip loosening on his sword, his hard features softening as he watched Kove's shoulders sag with defeat. Kove looked down at his sword, turning the hilt to inspect it, although, Ryon got the impression it was Kove's way of distracting himself from what he was about to say.

"I saw how much you cared about her," Kove continued. "Saw how much you were willing to give up for her...And I know that feeling. *Knew* that feeling. And in that moment, when my sword was sticking out of your chest, that's when I realised that in killing that human, I would have hurt you more than anyone else could."

Ryon blinked a few times, unsure if he imagined this entire conversation. Then as sure as if a switch had been pressed, Kove abruptly stood, shaking himself from any emotion. He sheathed his sword behind his back and lifted his chin. "So," he said, clearing his throat. "What's the plan?"

Ryon hesitated but then dropped his gaze to the bodies of the Reds that lay scattered, motionless, around them. If Kove wasn't willing to help, he wouldn't have come here and destroyed those Reds, ultimately saving Ryon's life. He lifted his wrist to see that he was already healing thanks to those two blood bags he'd just consumed.

Walking over to the nearest Red, he followed Kove's example and squatted down to wipe his sword on the male's shirt before looking up at Kove. "We're going to visit the King."

CHAPTER THIRTY

"What do you mean he was your boyfriend?" Laina demanded as Brynn's gaze went back to Zane, her expression one of pure shock.

"Ah yes, that was fun," Zane said smugly. Then his voice grew serious, "but I didn't appreciate being broken up with." After a moment, he asked, "did you get the little gift that I left for you in that alley in Oak Hills?"

Laina's blood turned cold, and she turned to look at Zane as Brynn walked forward.

"What are you talking about?" her sister asked, her voice tense, *strained*, as she stepped up to the glass wall where Zane stood on the other side.

The edges of Zane's lips curled up in a smile, causing Laina's stomach to churn. "I guess I should be thanking you. If I hadn't left you that little gift—well, *two* of them, in fact—the King would never have sought me out and invited me to join the Shadows." His smile widened. "He liked my work; said I had *potential*. And now, here I am at his right hand."

Brynn's hand whipped out and slammed the glass window

so fast that Laina jumped in reaction. "Fuck you!" *Slam.* "You *fucking* psychopath! I'll kill you!" *Slam. Slam. Slam.*

Zane threw his head back and laughed, then turned and walked away, flanked by the vampire from earlier.

Laina stood frozen, feeling as though her entire world had shifted. That closure Brynn had tried to help her find? Well, she'd just found it. Zane had murdered her parents. It was *Zane.* And it was all because...it was because of a breakup. A wave of emotions hit her. She felt overwhelmed, and her heart and stomach felt as though they'd plummeted to the floor.

Brynn let out something that sounded like a whimper, and Laina's eyes snapped up, not realising that she had begun to stare at the ground somewhere along the lines. Brynn remained standing against the glass wall, her hands by her side and her shoulders hunched. Laina watched as Brynn wrapped her arms around herself and hunched forward as if in pain.

"Brynn," Laina whispered, walking over to her. She turned her sister around and wrapped her arms around her. It took a minute, but Brynn's arms finally moved to embrace Laina in return.

"I didn't know he was..." she sobbed. *She didn't know he was a vampire?* "We only went out at night. I never saw him through the day, and his eyes...they weren't red back then." She sobbed harder, and Laina held her tighter. "I didn't know."

"It's not your fault. Brynn," Laina said, rubbing her sister's back. Laina was angry—devastatingly angry—and when she had spoken to Ryon about her parents, she had felt deep down that she blamed not only herself, but also Brynn for not being at dinner that night. But now? She realised blame was a pointless sensation. No one could control the actions of another, and Brynn wasn't to blame at all. *Zane* was the one to blame—no one else. "It's not your fault," Laina repeated.

Brynn pulled away abruptly, stepping back and lifting her chin as she swiped away the tears that had begun to run-down her face. "Crying won't bring them back." *And she's back.* Laina could pinpoint the moment Brynn's signature shell fell firmly back into place.

"You don't have to be strong right now. You know that don't you?" Laina said, watching as Brynn paced around the room, searching the corners, the walls. She *wished* her sister would let her guard down. She *wished* Brynn would finally take down those defensive walls and show some fear. Show some *humanity.* She knew it was in there. After Laina had read Brynn's text to their mother, she'd learned that deep down, Brynn was just as vulnerable as Laina was. But Laina's walls had never been quite so reinforced like Brynn's were. After their parents' deaths, Brynn had built a fortress around her heart whereas Laina only had a cage. Ryon had broken through that cage last night and now, as Laina watched Brynn search the room, she couldn't but wonder what it would possibly take to break through to Brynn.

"This has nothing to do with being strong or what either of us is feeling. We are in a *cell*, Laina," Brynn said, gesturing around the room. "We need to think logically. We need to figure out a way out of here."

Laina frowned as something on Brynn's arm caught her eye. Brynn lifted her arm to run a hand through her hair and it was then that Laina saw it—on her right elbow—at what peeked out from just under the sleeve of her shirt. A white bandage. She thought she'd noticed it when Brynn had been slamming the glass, but with what Zane had admitted to, she hadn't dwelled on it. "Brynn, your arm."

Laina rolled up the sleeve of her own sweatshirt to reveal a similar bandage on her elbow. *Blood.* "They're taking blood," she said, seeing Brynn staring down at her bandaged arm. They must have done it when they had been unconscious.

Laina made her way over to the bed and sat down before the anger, fear, and anxiousness caused her knees to give way. A scream echoed down the hallway, and Laina glanced out the glass wall, finally taking notice that there were more cells with glass walls opposite them. She stood and went to the glass, glancing down the hall to see movement at the end of it. She couldn't see exactly what was going on, only shadows of movement and then the slam of a door. When she raked her gaze over each cell, she noticed not far from them was an occupied one. A man with light brown hair sat on the bed, his eyes staring at the wall opposite him. They were glazed over, and he appeared to be in some kind of trance...just like the people in that hospital. Then her eyes drifted lower...to the bandage at his elbow. "They're keeping us for blood," she said, coming to the realisation. "To feed them."

"What?" Brynn asked, stopping her pacing. "Why? I mean, why *us*?"

Laina swung around to face her sister and inhaled deeply. It was time to tell Brynn everything. "I haven't exactly been honest with you."

When Brynn's brows drew together, Laina returned to her bed and sat down. It took a moment for Brynn to stop glaring at Laina and make her way across the room to sit on her own bed. Laina had a passing thought that this position—Laina on her bed and Brynn on hers—was exactly how they used to sit each night when they shared a room growing up. They used to talk for hours about nothing in particular. She shook her head. So much had changed. They weren't the same anymore. The *world* wasn't the same anymore.

"What's going on?" Brynn asked, leaning forward with her elbows on her knees.

Laina took in another breath. "Remember when you called me the other night when I was out with Max in that club?" Brynn nodded. "We ran into some...*trouble* in an alley." She heard Brynn's breath hitch, but she kept going. "We were all okay, but...that was the first time I learned vampires exist."

"The first time?" Brynn demanded. Laina took that moment to look up. Brynn's eyes were wide, her hands locked together, and her fingers entwined so tightly her knuckles were white.

Pursing her lips, Laina decided to keep all details about Ryon and Kove to herself. "I was at the gala too, with Max. I think that's why they took us...well, me. Because Max and I managed to escape."

Brynn stood up and began to pace again. "I'm trying, Laina." Her tone was filled with defeat and Laina didn't know whether to feel anger or guilt. "I'm really trying to be your big sister and take care of you but when you don't tell me any—"

Laina cut her off. "That's the problem, Brynn. I never asked you to take care of me." She pulled herself up to stand, trying to keep her voice calm. This wasn't the place to be having this conversation but then again, if not now, then when? It's not like they had anything else to do. "I-I don't need another mother."

Brynn swung around, her eyes flaring—both with anger and hurt, and Laina didn't know how to feel about that, but she continued anyway. "You've been smothering me, Brynn. You've been treating me like a child. Do you want to know why I haven't told you about this? Why I *don't* tell you things? Because *this* is how you react!"

"You're being ridiculous!" Brynn chided.

A surge of anger and frustration erupted inside of Laina. "Do you want to *know* how I made it out of the gala alive? Do you even *care?*"

"Of course, I care! I wouldn't be so worried about you if I didn't care!"

A burst of laughter exploded from Laina's mouth. "*This* is you being worried?" Brynn opened her mouth on a retort, but Laina didn't give her a chance. *Fuck it*, Laina thought. She'd put everything on the table. "Ryon. Ryon is the reason I didn't tell you. He's the one who helped us escape. He saved our lives."

"Who the *fuck* is Ryon?" Brynn demanded.

"He's a vampire," Laina answered and just as she'd wanted to, she really did put *everything* out on the table... "And I *love* him."

Laina only had time to see Brynn's mouth gape, her eyes wide with disbelief, before the sound of the cell door opening had them both turning around. A vampire Laina had never seen before stood in the doorway with his red eyes trained on her. "The King wants to see you."

CHAPTER THIRTY-ONE

"I've got him!" Kove called out from beside Ryon. The dozen or so vampires that guarded the front doors of the palace turned around, their red eyes darting between Ryon, Kove, and Kove's hand wrapped tightly around Ryon's arm. "You can let the King know that I have your male and he's willing to cooperate."

Ryon kept quiet, secretly willing Kove to remember the plan. As if reading his mind, Kove tightened his grip on Ryon's arm and gave it a knowing squeeze before they made their way up the stairs. The Reds glanced to one another but didn't ask any questions as they opened the doors and led them inside.

"I've already frisked him and removed his weapons. He's all yours," Kove said, meeting Ryon's gaze. Even though their eyes met for only a second, Ryon could see Kove's hesitancy. If the plan was successful, they would have nothing to worry about. But if something went wrong—and if Ryon were being honest, there was *a lot* that could go wrong—then there was a good chance Ryon and Kove would never see each other again.

Ryon watched as Kove disappeared down the hallway. He had explained the details of the lower level and told Kove that if Fynn and the others were being held captive, there was a good chance they would be down there.

Ryon snarled as rough hands grabbed his elbow, guiding him down the opposite hallway to where the dining hall was. He'd given Kove his jacket, holster, and blades, but left one small knife strapped to his ankle. And thanks to Kove telling those Reds that he wasn't armed, they didn't check for any weapons. His plan now was to see the King and keep him distracted until Kove found Fynn and the others, then they'd find a way to take the King down together.

When they reached the room, the Reds swung the door open, pushed him inside and closed it again. He stumbled forward and when he looked over to the long dining table, the breath caught in his throat. The Shadows—his *friends*—Fynn, Xavier, Malik, Rune, Damien, and Darick, were all seated at the table with a feast set out before them. But they weren't eating. Their backs were ramrod straight, their hands in their laps and their eyes...their eyes were wide and glazed over as they stared blankly at nothing. Almost as if they were...*compelled*.

A deep rumble of laughter dragged Ryon's attention away from his friends and over to the King seated at the head of the dining table. Unlike the frozen-in-place Shadows, the King had a plate full of food, and when his laughter died down, he picked up a nearby napkin and began to dab at his mouth.

"Did you know vampires can be compelled?" the King asked nonchalantly. "Of course, only those with Royal blood have the ability to do so, but it does come in handy."

Ryon snarled as rage tore through him. The King was

playing games with his friends...with their *minds*. *Fuck* buying time for Kove to come back—the plan wouldn't work now, anyway. He'd have to do this himself. Without another thought, he faded behind the King's chair and threw out his hands to wrap around—

But the King was gone.

A tsking sound came from beside him as his eyes dropped to the empty chair.

"Predictable," the King drawled as he moved to the next chair and pulled it out. "Please, sit," Ryon responded by pulling his lip back on a snarl, but the King just raised a brow. "I'm going to ignore this behaviour since I am aware that you're merely retaliating over the capture of your friends. However, if you do not sit down, I will *make you*." The King's fangs lengthened, and Ryon hesitated before sitting down.

"Better," the King said as he took up the chair at the top of the table once more. Ryon couldn't help but notice he wasn't wearing his usual garb. He still wore that golden crown, but instead of the formal red suit jacket, he now wore a red velvet robe that hung down to the ground with the Royal crest on his shoulder. That crest...Ryon narrowed his eyes on it. He'd seen it somewhere before...

"The ability to compel other vampires has served me well in my long life. Did you know that vampires actually do retain all of their memories from their human life?" Ryon's eyes snapped up to the King's as he continued. "The transition does not wipe their mind. No, that is done by their maker to ensure they don't try to escape and go back to the human world."

Ryon's eyes widened, but before he could wrap his head around that, the King went on. "*But* do you know what's *most* interesting about the transition from human to vampire? I've discovered that if you withhold blood from a newly transitioned vampire for a day or two, you can almost guarantee that they will be lost to their blood lust, permanently—and then it's much easier to compel them to follow me."

That's how the King had formed an army of Reds. By *starving* them after the transition. Ryon suspected the Red's had been compelled but now he knew the truth. He clenched his teeth. "What the *fuck* is wrong with you?"

The King let out a chuckle and picked up the gold chalice from the table before leaning back in his chair. He ignored Ryon's question and closed his eyes, inhaling from the chalice, swishing it around and moaning before he opened his eyes. "Don't you just love the taste of *fresh* blood? Would you care for some?" The King held it out for him, but Ryon shook his head. He had no interest in—

Panic seized Ryon's chest when the King pulled the chalice back, and a familiar scent suddenly struck his senses. A scent that couldn't possibly be anywhere in the vicinity of this palace. Ryon pushed aside the thoughts and calmed his racing heart. *She's safe. And nowhere near here.*

"You must be wondering why I've been searching for you," the King said, interrupting Ryon's train of thought.

Ryon glanced up to see the King's now brown eyes on him. He'd never taken notice of the colour before, but it was a light brown, not unlike his own. Ryon had only ever seen the King a few times before, and both times, the King's eyes had burned with gold. He shrugged, feigning nonchalance. "I assume it has something to do with calling you a coward and fading out of your grasp at the gala."

"Yes...and no," the King said. "Where do you stand on the war against the humans?"

Ryon shook his head, not understanding where the King was going with the question. "I stand nowhere. War is unnecessary."

"And why is that?" The King cocked his head to the side. "Because you care so much for them?" he said, and Ryon didn't miss the judgement in his tone.

Act like you don't care. "I don't care for humans other than their blood. But I don't think they need to die, either."

"Is that why you freed those two humans last night?"

A sliver of fear crept into Ryon's chest, but he ignored it and shrugged, sitting back in his own chair, and hoping he looked more uncaring than he felt. The King picked up the chalice and took a sip before placing it down again. Ryon's eyes stayed on that chalice before the King's words snapped his attention back to him. "So, you don't care for humans? Not even that female in the black dress last night?"

That fear increased tenfold, but he stifled it, managing to stay slouched in the chair. "No, I don't care for her."

"Hmm," the King mused, leaning his elbow on the table as he stared at Ryon. "Very well." The King sat back again. "I admit, I let my anger get the better of me when I saw you... show *mercy* to those humans, and it appears..." the King's gaze raked over Ryon's shoulders, "...that you have healed despite your injuries. *Good.*" The King sat forward, and Ryon felt the heavy weight of his stare. "Because I am willing to give you another chance."

At Ryon's questioning glance, the King said, "I have a legacy to uphold here in Ladwick—and the entire Garabitha region. One that I'm hoping you will maintain."

"Why should I care about your legacy? What does it have to do with me?"

"It has everything to do with you, *boy*." That word again. "Soran kept you hidden from me for too long."

"What the *fuck* are you talking about?" Ryon spat, glaring at the King. He was done with these riddles. "Where *is* Soran? What did you do to him?"

The King waved a hand dismissively. "He's dead. But you don't need to worry about that." Pure rage roiled through Ryon, but he tapped it down, suddenly aware of Zane—the *traitor*—and half a dozen Reds in the corner of the room. It would do Ryon no favours if he lashed out right now. "You are strong—I see it," the King continued, "and you have potential...Once you get past your sympathy for humans."

"I told you, I don't care about humans," Ryon snapped. "I just don't see the point in killing them."

The King stared at Ryon for a long moment before he abruptly picked up his chalice and took a sip, licking his lips when he pulled it away. "Are you sure you wouldn't like to try some?" He leaned forward and placed the chalice directly in front of Ryon. "I think you'll thoroughly enjoy it."

Ryon frowned. Why was the King pushing this so much? A sudden scent of vanilla, cinnamon...and rose struck him. *No. No, it can't be.* His heart twisted with terror, and he barely managed to keep from fading over to the King and tearing his throat out. But he needed to stay calm. He needed to bide his time. *It's not Laina's blood. It's not Laina's blood.*

"Or would you prefer to drink it straight from the source?" Ryon's eyes snapped to the King's, his chest constricting with panic. *No. Laina can't be here. She can't.* The King turned to someone behind him and motioned for something before returning his gaze to Ryon. "After all, if you don't care for humans—and you don't care for that woman from last night—you wouldn't mind if I bring her in to feed my battalion. Because they *do* prefer to drink straight from the source."

CHAPTER THIRTY-TWO

E very step Laina took felt like she was getting closer to
death as two vampires guided her down a long, darkened hallway. Her heart was lodged firmly in her throat as they
guided her up staircase after staircase and hallway after hallway
until they reached a closed door. *This is it*, she thought as they
pushed the door open and ushered her inside. Her palms were
sweaty, her head was pounding in time with her heart, and she
felt on the verge of passing out, but she lifted her chin and
steeled herself. It took her a moment to realise she was
standing in a dining room. Her gaze drifted over the dining
table—there were some males sitting rigidly down one end
and on the other end was—

Ryon. It was Ryon. Except...he had his back to her. He
didn't even glance over his shoulder as the door slammed shut
and she jumped in response. Laina's gaze drifted to the male
sitting beside Ryon. She recognised him as the vampire from
the stage at the gala last night. But now he wore a gold crown,
and instead of the red velvet suit jacket, he wore a black outfit
underneath a red velvet robe. *The King. He's the King.* And

was smiling widely at her as if she'd just been presented to him as a gift.

Laina's gaze drifted back to Ryon as he glanced uncaringly over his shoulder. But then he turned back to the table before their eyes could meet. He was casually slouched in his chair with his arm resting on the table. That scarred hand of his that had been so gentle with her only hours ago, was outstretched, playing with the fork in front of him as if he had nothing better to do. For all intents and purposes, he looked like he didn't have a care in the world...but Laina could see the tense strain of those muscles underneath the thin t-shirt he wore. Was he...pretending not to care?

Her eyes darted to the smiling King and then back to Ryon. And it was then that realisation struck her. The King had been the one to snap those arrows into his back. '*A warning*,' Ryon had said. Was this his punishment? Kidnapping her? And was Ryon feigning carelessness so that the King would leave her alone?

Laina's mouth betrayed her mind when his name left her lips. "Ryon?" she whispered.

The King's smile widened, and he glanced to Ryon...but Ryon didn't turn around. He didn't even flinch.

"I thought you didn't care about her?" the King asked Ryon. "She seems to care about you," he added. Laina swayed on her feet at the King's words, but she inwardly shook herself. *It's all a ploy. It's part of the plan. Ryon has a plan.*

She watched the back of Ryon's head as he shrugged and glanced at the King. "I sated my needs with her, that's all." Laina's breath left her at the hurt those words caused. *It's all a ploy*, she reminded herself. *Yes. Yes, it has to be.* But those words...*God,* how they'd hurt.

She stayed quiet but the King's gaze narrowed on her before darting back to Ryon. She had tried to maintain her composure, she had tried to keep a straight face but then the King said, "it appears she didn't get the message."

Ryon sighed and turned around, facing her for the first time. Her heart fluttered for a split-second then plummeted to the floor at his expression. His features were pulled tight on a frown, and he looked...*frustrated*. And suddenly she couldn't tell if he was faking it or not. She thought she'd be able to decipher what his plan was from his eyes, but they held no emotion. No affection. *Nothing*. And then he spoke.

"It meant nothing, okay?" His voice was flat, even, and completely void of any feeling whatsoever. Laina's heart felt as though it were bleeding out on the floor, while she remained frozen in place, confused. She searched his eyes for some kind of hint that this wasn't real. That his *words* weren't true...but just like before, she found nothing.

His broad shoulders lifted in a shrug. "It was a bit of give and take, just like all the other humans I've been with. You're not special, and you're delusional if you ever thought you were."

Laina could almost hear the *crack* as her heart split in two. Her knees weakened as she realised the truth. Ryon wasn't faking it now—he'd been faking it with *her*. His eyes held no emotion, his tone didn't waver, and he looked her in the eye and told her it had all been...*a bit of give and take*. Why would he say that? Why would he use *those* words if...if he was faking it?

The King's roar of laughter echoed through the room as Ryon turned back to the table. *It had all been a lie.* Laina was going to be sick. She was going to be *sick*. Her hand flew to her stomach as if by doing so, she could prevent herself from retching. *It had all been a lie.*

When the King's laughter died off, Ryon glanced over at him. "I think you need to feed your battalion with another human. This one seems too emotional."

"Ah, but you see, that just makes it more *fun*." The King waved someone over, but Laina's eyes were riveted to Ryon as he turned back to playing with that fork again.

Laina screamed as rough hands suddenly appeared on her —pulling her backwards by her arms, shoulders, waist. She stumbled, panic seizing her as the hands loosened, allowing her to catch herself before she fell. Panting, she looked up to see four vampires with red eyes smiling down at her—and at the back of them stood Zane. "S-Stop," she said, her voice cracking with fear. Someone came up behind her and yanked at her hair, causing her to scream again and her hair to fall out from the bun it was tied into. Zane and the four vampires closed in on her once more, crowding her until she couldn't see the dining table, the King...or Ryon.

"Ryon!" she screamed, no longer caring if it was a ruse or not. He'd saved her life before. Would he save her again?

No reply.

The surrounding vampires chuckled, and she heard the King say, "Do stop playing with your food, gentle males," his own voice filled with amusement.

"Ryon!" she shrieked as they stepped in further, grabbing her arms with lightning speed.

Her breaths were ragged, her throat sore from the screaming and her body thrumming with aches from where the vampires were tugging and yanking at her. "No!" she yelled as the two vampires that held her arms peeled back their lips on a snarl. Her eyes widened as she realised what was happening. Their fangs lengthened as they lifted her wrists to their mouths. *No. no!* She screamed and tried to fight their hold, but it was useless. She cried out when she felt another vampire behind her, pushing her hair to the side before she felt warm breath against her neck. *This is how I die. Drained of blood, just like my parents. This is it.* Tears welled, and she squeezed her eyes shut, crying out when she felt sharp fangs pierce her wrists.

And then *chaos.*

Laina swayed and flung open her eyes when shouts broke out around her. She could no longer feel hands holding back her wrists and shoulders and it took a moment for her brain to catch up with the scenes before her. Three vampires were forcibly restraining Ryon, holding him back by the arms and neck as he panted heavily. His eyes flared with gold as they locked on her. She glanced down to see a vampire getting off the floor, red marks around his neck as if someone had wrapped their hands around him. *Had Ryon done that?* She was so confused. She pushed down the hope that it had all been a ruse after all as someone began clapping. Laina glanced over as the King slowly stood from where he'd remained seated at the dining table. He strode towards them as he continued to clap, his face looking anything but congratulatory.

"That was almost believable. *Almost.*" The King sneered as Ryon finally tore his gaze from Laina to look at him. "Too bad you have just shown me your weakness, boy." Ryon's eyes widened as he glanced from the King to Laina and back to the King, the fear in them unmistakable. *Did he mean...Oh God. No.*

"And if you're going to inherit my Kingdom, my *legacy*,

one day," the King began. Laina cried out when she felt hands on either side of her head, holding firmly. The King had disappeared from where he'd been standing beside Ryon—and by the way Ryon's eyes flared when he looked over her shoulder —she knew the King was now behind her. Laina sucked in a breath, her heart sinking to the ground when she heard the King's voice, loud against her ear. "I need to remove what makes you *weak*."

Ryon thrashed wildly against the three—now four vampires—who held him back, his eyes locked on hers with a silent apology. Laina screamed as she felt a sudden tugging pressure on her head, followed by a deafening *crack* that began at her neck and reverberated through her entire body. She was vaguely aware of a feeling of utter numbness as she fell to the ground in a heap. Just before her vision turned to black.

CHAPTER THIRTY-THREE

As soon as the Reds loosened their hold on Ryon, he faded to Laina, catching her before she fell to the ground. *No. No. No!* Her head lay to the side, her mouth slightly open and her eyes closed. He could sense a faint heartbeat, but he knew it wouldn't be long.

"I-I'm sorry," he whispered, his voice cracking as his heart felt as though it were collapsing in on itself. "I'm so sorry." His words turned to a whimper as he closed his eyes and folded himself over her, wanting to feel her close. Ryon's gut twisted with regret and sorrow as he recalled the horrible things he'd said to her in front of the King—because of the King. Ryon had only been trying to act disinterested to make the King disinterested...but in the end, it made no difference.

He let out a choked sound as he remembered how hurt she looked when he'd finally turned around to face her. He'd willed her to see through the words, but in the end, she had died believing that he didn't care for her when the truth was, he felt so much more than that. He...he had come to *love* her.

The sound of a door closing had Ryon glancing up to see the King and all the Reds had gone, leaving him with Laina and the still-frozen Shadow members. He glanced down at Laina, at her soft hair, her long eyelashes, her petite nose, her parted lips...A flicker of hope crept into his chest. *Maybe... Maybe it's not too late. Maybe I can still heal her...somehow.* He wasn't sure how a broken neck could heal exactly but he had to try. He *had* to.

Without another thought, Ryon lifted his wrist and bit into the flesh with his fangs before lowering it over her mouth. With her lips parted slightly; he hoped that if enough blood dripped into her throat, her body would find a way to mend itself. The breath caught in his throat when he noticed her heartbeat was fainter now...but she was still alive, which meant there was still hope. *Come on! Come on!* He lifted his wrist, but the drips of blood on her lips told him it wasn't enough. He pierced his skin again...and again, creating more puncture wounds that now dripped blood in a continuous flow down his arm. He held onto that minuscule glimmer of hope as he placed his wrist over her mouth and threw his head back, praying to the human God to spare Laina's life. He stayed there for what could have been hours, just holding Laina's limp form and hoping his blood was doing enough. *Please. Please! For fuck's sake, please!*

Silence. Ryon had been so lost in his thoughts that he hadn't noticed how silent the room was. He glanced down and sucked in a breath when he recognised the newfound silence was coming from Laina. Her heart had *stopped*. He didn't need to check her pulse to know it, but still, he pressed a finger to her neck. *Nothing.* Ryon stared, frozen and emotionless, as the best thing to ever happen to him slipped from his fingers. *Gone.* She was...*gone.* Laina had been the sun in his night. The dark to his light. And what good was the dark without the light?

He threw his head back and roared as grief and uncontrollable rage exploded through him, causing tendrils of seething fury to reverberate through every fibre in his being. The King did this. The King killed Laina because he said she made him *weak,* but Ryon was about to show him exactly how *weak* he could be. Ryon planted one last kiss on Laina's forehead, memorising the feel of her skin on his lips, before he gently lowered her body to the floor. Then he was running. He yanked open the door, his vision red with anger as he ran down the hallway and up the stairs. He could scent the King was near, and when he reached the top of the stairs, he saw him.

Ryon faded to the King in a blur, pinning him against the wall by the throat, his anger fuelling his strength and speed like never before. The unsuspecting King let out a strangled sound as Ryon felt hands on him—likely the Reds or Zane—in an attempt to pull him back. But Ryon wasn't letting go.

"You *killed* her," Ryon spat.

The King choked out a laugh. "Grieving, over a human?"

"She's more than a human to me," Ryon hissed, squeezing his hand tighter over the King's throat. The King made a choking sound, and the Reds redoubled their effort to pull Ryon off him, but Ryon held firm. The King jerked his head to warn the Reds away, and they stepped back, unhanding Ryon. Clearly, he thought he could take on Ryon himself...*Stupid King.* Ryon pulled the King away from the wall only to slam him back again.

The King grunted with the impact as he tried to fight Ryon's hold—but Ryon didn't budge. His rage, his fury, and his grief were fuelling his strength and he wouldn't let go until he crushed the King's throat and watched him run out of oxygen. Ryon knew the King deserved a much slower, torturous death but right now, with the overwhelming emotions running through him, he wasn't capable of doing anything else.

A heartbeat passed before the King's brows drew low and he sneered. "I was wrong about you. You *are* weak even without that pitiful human! Now I realise—" The King let out a strangled sound and tried again. "T-that you are not worthy of the blood that runs through your veins!"

"What the *fuck* are you talking about?" Ryon demanded as confusion roiled with rage inside him. The King was *fucking* crazy and ever since Ryon had stepped foot inside that dining room downstairs, he'd spoken in riddles. And Ryon was done with it.

He pulled the King back and slammed him into the wall. The King hissed, his fingernails digging into Ryon's arm—but Ryon wouldn't let up. He slammed him again.

"H-How do you think you got those scars?" The King choked out, his gaze dropping to Ryon's scarred hand. "It was because you were *weak*! Prepared to run into the sun." The King's laugh echoed around the open lobby. "P-Prepared to chase your mother out into the sun like a good little boy—" The King's words broke off into a cough.

Ryon frowned and shook his head. His fingers twitched against the King's throat and the King took advantage of it, pushing Ryon off with a force that sent him stumbling back to the handrail of the stairs. The King stalked forward but Ryon couldn't process what was happening, his mind in turmoil. How did the King know about his dream? He'd only told Fynn, and even then, he hadn't mentioned any details. But... but in the dream he was a young vampire—which was impossible since he'd transitioned into a vampire as an adult. Hadn't he?

"You were meant to be a fearless leader for our kind," the King snarled, making Ryon's head snap up to meet his gaze. The King stood before him but made no move to retaliate. "You could have been powerful, but *she* took you. She took you, and she made you *weak*!"

"Who?" Ryon demanded, his stomach churning as pieces of the puzzle that was his life began to appear. *Is he talking about my...mother?* And if—*somehow*—that dream was in fact memory, what did Ryon's mother have to do with the King? But no, none of that made sense. The only way that dream could have been a memory would be if he was...if he was *born*. And that was impossible because the only vampire's that were born were...*Royalty.*

Ryon's eyes widened on the King as more puzzle pieces fell into place. That strong jaw and straight nose...was just like his own. The thick eyebrows, light brown eyes, and dark hair... just like his own. He thought back to Fynn in the hallway as he looked up at the portrait of the King, '*you look like him*', he'd said. How had he missed it all?

The King's lip curled back on a snarl and his eyes turned pure gold. "It's time you remember, *Ryszard*!"

Ryon's hand flew up to his head as an intense, sharp pain exploded through his temple. *Remember.* The word triggered something inside of him as a rush of information overwhelmed him, causing both hands to fly to his head. Images rocked his mind. And thoughts. And feelings. And emotions. He saw the woman from his dream, and he knew suddenly, without a shadow of a doubt, that she was his *mother*. He had loved her, and she'd loved him. She'd birthed him—a vampire. He had been...*born*. Ryon remembered sitting with his mother in a small cottage—the same one from the dream. He remembered her telling him about the King of the vampires who would one day be superseded by someone better—by someone who cared for more than just themselves. *You're better than him.* His mother's words returned to him with newfound meaning as he recalled something else...Her panic. He remembered his mother frantically writing something down on a piece of paper before stuffing it under the floorboards. She knew they were going to be attacked. That night, someone came to visit their small cottage—*Soran*. It was Soran. His mother had pleaded with Soran that if anything were to happen to her, he was to take Ryon and keep his identity a secret. That he was to *'protect the heir to the throne'*.

The King continued to speak, but Ryon wasn't listening as his thoughts turned from shock and disbelief to seething anger. Everything he'd known...everything he'd believed...his entire *existence* as a vampire had been a *lie*. And he'd lived that lie, right under the nose of the King who'd ultimately put him there. That red robe...the way the King referred to him as '*boy*', even that damn crest, embroidered with the initials C and D. It had all felt familiar to him, but he hadn't pieced it all together until now.

And then he gasped as he realised *why*—why he hadn't been able to remember anything. He'd been...*compelled*. The King had compelled him to forget. Ryon dropped his gaze to the scars that ran up his hand to his wrist. The proof that it was real. It was *all* real.

A fresh surge of anger ran through him as the realisations continued. The King had killed his mother. He'd killed Soran...and he'd killed Laina. He'd killed *everyone* Ryon had ever loved. And it didn't matter that the King was the one who had sired him—the King needed to die, regardless.

Ryon's instinct beckoned him to move, and he did. Before his mind would catch up, he slammed the King against the wall. In one swift move, and with a speed he'd never managed before, he pulled out the small knife strapped to his ankle and plunged it into the King's heart. The King's eyes widened as his hands flew up, tugging and clawing at Ryon's arms. More hands were tugging at him now—the Red's attempting to pull him off the King. But Ryon wasn't done. Leaving the knife wedged in the King's chest, he pulled his hand back and thrust it forward, pushing the hilt further in.

"This is for my *mother*," Ryon spat, pushing the knife in some more. "This is for Soran." Ryon pushed the knife in again, his own chest aching with the grief of naming those he cared about. "And this is for *Laina*," he hissed as he slammed his hand down on the hilt until it no longer sat outside of the King's body.

Ryon slowly stepped back...and so did the Reds that were attempting to pull him away. Blood began to trickle from the King's mouth before he fell forward onto his knees, then dropped to the floor. In a daze and panting, he turned around to see every Red now stood, tense and staring at him. Zane stood at the top of the staircase, his eyes darting between Ryon and the King and back again—then he ran for the front entrance. Ryon considered chasing him, but he had a room full of Reds to deal with. A heartbeat passed, and he waited for them to attack. And waited. When they didn't move, he looked around at their wide, red eyes and noticed they appeared to be awaiting instructions. *Ryszard. The heir to the throne. The blood that runs through your veins.* He was...their King now, wasn't he? His father's words came back to him. *Vampires can be compelled—only those with Royal blood have the ability to do so.*

"From this moment on, you will not kill another human," he called out to them, not knowing exactly how they would react. The Reds' eyes glazed over, and they went rigid, and he let out the breath he didn't realise he'd been holding. His... father's compulsion on them must have broken when he died —Ryon could compel them now. "I reinstate the rules that King Cazimir revoked. You will *never* kill a human and if you do, you will suffer the punishment of death!" After a moment's hesitation, he glanced around at their wide-eyed stares. "Now go," he added. The Reds nodded and one by one, they began to disperse to wherever it was the King had put them up.

A door slammed somewhere in the distance, footsteps echoing down the hallway, until Fynn exploded into the room, panting and wide-eyed.

"Fynn?" Ryon asked, rushing down the stairs. The King's death must have broken their compulsion too. "Are you okay? The others?"

Fynn nodded absentmindedly, his gaze darting between the Reds that were leaving the room and the King's body. "What the hell—" he stopped himself, shaking his head. "No time, you need to hurry. Dining hall—*now*."

"What?" Ryon's mind couldn't process what was going

on, his brain was still catching up from the last five minutes, but then Fynn's lips moved.

One word. One word was all Fynn said before Ryon was moving at a dead run past Fynn and down the hallway to where the dining hall was. One word.

"Laina."

CHAPTER THIRTY-FOUR

Laina was catapulted from the most peaceful sleep she'd ever had to a frenzied hunger she'd never experienced before. She felt as though she was caught in a haze as she gasped for breath and opened her eyes. *So hungry. So damn hungry.*

A large black chandelier hung above her, and she frowned. *Where was—*

Patches of memories came back to her like a broken movie reel. *Brynn. The dining room. Ryon. The King twisting her neck.*

Oh, God. Was she...*dead?* No, she couldn't be. She glanced around. She was still in the dining room. And goddammit, she was hungry. She sat up so fast her head began to spin. She groaned and closed her eyes, pinching her forehead. *What happened?* Opening her eyes, she pushed herself up to stand... and stopped when her gaze landed on six large males, all wearing black leather jackets and looking back at her with wide eyes. *What are they looking at?*

Hunger pains shot through her, making her double over in

pain, but then a scent...a most *delicious* scent, reached her. *What is that?* She closed her eyes and inhaled. With her eyes closed like this, she inadvertently focused on her senses, realising that she could hear those males' heartbeats. All *six* of them. And that smell...

She flung her eyes open as a primal urge she'd never felt before came over her. Her body acted of its own accord, and she peeled back her lips, letting out a vicious snarl. And then she moved. She had no idea how she moved so fast, but all she knew was that one, if not all, of these males, had something she wanted. *Blood.* One moment she was standing beside the dining table. The next, she was pushing one of the males back against the far back wall and staring down at the pulsing vein at his neck.

"Ah, little help here, guys," the male said as he lifted his hands in surrender. What the hell was she doing? She recoiled somewhat, but her body wouldn't cooperate. The aching hunger inside her wanted—no, it *needed*—to feed. She felt an itching sensation at her gums, and she opened her mouth wide on impulse—

"Leave us!"

The instant she heard Ryon's voice, she stopped. *Ryon.* As if a bucket of freezing cold water had been poured over her head, her mind came crashing back to reality. *What am I doing?* Laina took a step back. And another. And another. She didn't realise she was still backing up until her back hit the dining table. She slowly lifted her hands to her mouth in a daze and felt...Fangs. She had *fangs*.

The sound of a door closing had her head snapping up. They were alone. Ryon slowly walked forward, his hands out, palms down as if trying to calm a rabid animal. *Was she the rabid animal?*

"Laina?" he asked gently. "*Fuck*, I thought I'd lost you." His words came out on a sigh, and she could practically see the relief rolling off him. *Lost me?* She couldn't understand what was happening but all she knew was that she was famished, and she felt as though she would die if she didn't get what she needed.

"I'm...I'm so...hungry," Laina's voice was croaky, her mouth dry, and when she caught the scent of blood again, she hunched over with a groan.

She felt Ryon's hands on her shoulders, and she sucked in a breath at their warmth. The sensation against her skin—even through her sweatshirt—only seemed to heighten her senses even more. And from this close, that scent...*Oh God*, that scent.

"Laina, look at me." She glanced up to see those light brown eyes widen before they flickered with gold. "I..." he started. "I need you to know everything I said in front of the King..." he shook his head. "I thought it would deter him from..." She watched as his throat bobbed on another swallow, making her gums itch to pierce that skin. Even through the hunger, she knew what he was saying. She *knew* he hadn't meant what he'd said—she knew it the moment he'd stopped those vampires from feeding on her. Ryon seemed to have noticed her eyes on his neck. He gave a quick shake of his head. "I'll explain everything later, but right now, you need to feed."

He tilted his head to the side, exposing his neck. She sucked in a breath as her eyes riveted to that vein that she knew would sate her hunger. "Human blood will keep you fulfilled for longer but—"

Laina plunged her fangs into his neck without another thought. Ryon grunted, and the sound sent vibrations through her body as the warm and intoxicating taste of his blood trickled down her throat.

She swallowed on a moan as Ryon lifted her onto the dining table and cupped the back of her head, holding her to his neck. Her thoughts became clearer with each swallow, and that haziness in her mind evaporated until all she could think about was how heightened her senses were...and how intimate the position was. As if Ryon was thinking the same, his free hand moved down to the small of her back and pulled her forward, into him. She let out a moan against his neck as her breasts flattened against his chest and she could feel his thick length against her stomach. *More.* She wanted *more.*

Her hands left his shoulders and moved to the fly of his jeans as she continued to drink from him. There would be nothing slow about this. This was all about primal, animalistic need and satisfaction. With Ryon's help, she unzipped his fly and shoved his jeans down his hips as his steel-hard erection sprang free. She released his neck long enough to frantically unzip her own jeans, and he lifted her up so she could shuffle out of her pants and underwear, leaving her bare to him.

"Bite me," he snarled, his eyes glowing bright gold.

His words sent a rush of desire through her, fuelling the need to taste him, feel him, have him. He lifted her completely off the table and shuffled backwards as Laina bit into his neck once more, eliciting a low moan from him. She felt him sit back on a chair and she didn't hesitate. She lifted her head from his neck and lowered her legs on either side of the chair, moving forward until she hovered over his engorged arousal.

"Bite me and *fuck* me, Laina." His voice was demanding and filled with a desperation that matched her own. "I need to feel you," he said.

Words escaped her and all inhibition vanished as she plunged her fangs into his neck once more and slid herself down over his shaft. She gasped into his neck at the delicious sensation of Ryon filling her up and stretching her.

Ryon let out a curse as one hand went to cupping the back of her head, the other squeezing her hip. She began to move, lifting herself up and lowering onto him as she continued to tug at his flesh, each swallow sending tendrils of pleasure and desire throughout her body, ending in an explosion of heat at her core. They were moving now and Laina had no idea how she managed to stay locked onto his neck, but she did. And the idea of having him inside of her every which way like this was sending her spiralling towards a release. Ryon was panting now as he took control, lifting her up and slamming her down over him, riding him.

The hunger pains dissipated, replaced with the all-consuming building pressure. Laina's body thrummed with the need to explode, teetering on the edge of control. She groaned and released his neck, running her tongue over it to close the wounds like she'd seen him do to her wrist. She threw her head back as their bodies met faster and faster, moving closer to a crescendo of desperate need and pleasure. Ryon lifted her up and thrust her down hard then moved his hand between her legs, his thumb finding her throbbing core, circling it, and sending her crashing over the edge. Stars appeared behind her eyes, and she cried out his name on her release. Ryon grunted as he slammed her down against him once more. He cursed and threw his own head back, saying her name like a prayer as he went rigid beneath her.

Long moments passed before muscular hands cupped her cheeks and guided her forehead to his. They held that position for what could have been moments or hours, Laina had no idea. But it felt right. Despite everything, being here with Ryon felt...*right.*

Once they both caught their breaths, he lifted his head and pressed a soft, lingering kiss on her lips. When he pulled back, he didn't go far. He held her face as their eyes met, and Laina was surprised to know that even as a vampire, the butterflies that had previously fluttered around in her stomach were alive and well.

"I thought you'd died. I thought I'd lost you," he whispered, giving her another kiss. When he pulled back, the intensity in his eyes turned those butterflies into hummingbirds. "I love you," he said, softly.

Laina's breath left her in a rush at his words. It took a moment to calm her racing heart enough for her to finally admit her own feelings for him. "I love you, too."

The smile that graced Ryon's lips made her itch to press another kiss there—and she did. When she pulled back, his smile widened before those brows of his dropped. "But just so you know, I'm going to pretend that you never tried to feed from Xavier," there was a playfulness in his tone, and she couldn't help but let out a chuckle.

BANG. BANG. BANG

"You do not want to go in there."

Laina tensed when she heard Kove's voice on the other side of the door. *Kove.* Her eyes darted to the door, and as if

Ryon knew what she was thinking, he said, "it's okay. He won't hurt you. He's...changed." She wished she could believe him, but that remained to be seen. Then she heard another voice.

"Like *hell* I don't want to go in there! My sister's in there!" *BANG. BANG. BANG.*

Brynn. Laina let out a curse as she climbed off Ryon and hastily pulled on her jeans. Her heart was hammering away inside her chest as relief warred with apprehension at seeing her sister. How would Brynn react to what she'd become?

Laina was vaguely aware of Ryon pulling his jeans over his hips when the door exploded open and a very angry looking Brynn stormed in, followed by a very angry looking Kove. When Laina's gaze landed on Kove, the breath caught in her throat. He'd tried to kill her, and she wouldn't get past that in a hurry. Even if they were the same species now.

Movement in the doorway caught her attention. She looked over to see the males in the leather jackets from earlier now piling into the room. Her cheeks heated, and she sent the one she'd attempted to bite an apologetic glance.

"My God, Laina!" Brynn rushed forward, snapping Laina's attention back to her sister. "Are you okay?" she asked, her gaze jumping all over Laina's body, looking for any hint of an injury. But she wouldn't find any.

"I tried to stop her," Kove said to Ryon, gesturing to Brynn. "But the frustrating *human* wouldn't listen, and I didn't think it would be wise to compel her." Brynn glared at Kove before looking back to Laina.

"I'm fine, really—" Laina's words died in her throat as she caught the first scent of blood—*human* blood. She stepped back as Brynn rushed forward and threw her arms around her in a hug. Laina closed her eyes and tried to appreciate the moment, but that delicious scent returned to her.

"Easy there," Ryon said, appearing at her side.

Brynn pulled back from the hug, realising Laina wasn't hugging her back. But it was too late. Laina peeled back her lips and hissed as her gums did that itching thing again. Were they...lengthening?

"Stupid human," Kove mumbled as he took Brynn's arm and began to guide her away. Laina could feel Brynn's wide eyes locked on her fangs, a look of realisation across her face.

"What happened to you?" Brynn said on a breath, the disbelief evident in her tone. "What the hell happened to you?"

"It's the human blood," Ryon whispered to Laina as she fought back the urge to attack her own sister. She clenched and unclenched her hands as Ryon's hand came around her waist. "You've taken enough from me to sate your needs for the moment, but not for long. You'll have to build up the resilience."

"You're one of them now, aren't you?" Brynn demanded, her eyes darting from Ryon back to Laina.

"Looks like it," Kove said. "Now, let's go before you become her next meal." He reached for Brynn's arm, but she stepped out of his grasp.

"Don't fucking touch me!" Brynn said.

"Yeah, well, I don't want to touch you either," Kove spat back.

"The King killed me," Laina said, interrupting Kove and Brynn. She couldn't believe what she was saying. It all felt so surreal. "Ryon..." she glanced over at him before turning back to Brynn. "He brought me back."

Brynn's eyes widened, and Laina could see her trying to piece it all together. After a moment of head shaking, swallowing, and eyes darting between Ryon and Laina, Brynn's lips thinned in reluctant acceptance. Then, as if suddenly recalling something, she glanced behind her at the males—then around the room.

"Where's Zane?" Brynn asked. *Zane.* Laina's ex-boyfriend and the one who'd killed their parents. He'd been in the room earlier—

"He ran, like the coward he is," Ryon said. *What?* Laina's head snapped to Ryon as his brows lowered in confusion. "Why do you ask?"

"Because he killed our parents. And now I'm going to kill *him*," Brynn said, her chin lifted defiantly as if she wasn't facing off an entire room of vampires.

"I'm going to help you," Laina added.

"We all will," Ryon said looking between Brynn and Laina, his voice unwavering as if making an oath. "We'll find him."

Brynn nodded before Kove took her arm again. Brynn yanked it back and glanced at Laina once more. "If there's no more danger here, then I...I'll come back tomorrow to check on you," she said. Then she turned and strode for the door. Laina had to stifle a grin when the males abruptly stepped to the side, rushing to make way for Brynn to leave the room, with a cursing Kove following her.

The tension in Laina's body left her when she could no longer scent human blood. When the urge to feed was no longer at the forefront of her mind. She watched as the males —who she assumed were the rest of the Shadows—filed out of the room.

"Wait!" she called out abruptly as the last one was about to leave.

He swung around. He looked so...*familiar*. "I've seen you somewhere before," she said, more to herself than to anyone else. At the Gala? *No. No, that wasn't it.* There was something about him that seemed so familiar. She took in his spiked up light brown hair, pale blue eyes, and groomed goatee. She'd *definitely* seen him before, but she couldn't pinpoint where. She shook her head. "Never mind."

He shrugged, pulling out a packet of cigarettes from his pocket before he followed the others out of the room, leaving Laina and Ryon alone once more.

"She'll be alright," Ryon said, turning Laina to him. He put his hands on her hips and pulled her closer to him. "Your sister will be alright. We'll find Zane. We'll find him and make him pay—all of us, together." Laina's shoulders sagged at the comfort those words brought. The *closure*. "Everything will be alright," he said.

"Everything will be alright," Laina repeated. She closed her eyes and let herself relax into Ryon's embrace. There was so much she needed to figure out, about her life and about everything now that she was...well, a *vampire*. But as a wave of overwhelming tiredness came over her, she realised all of that could wait until tomorrow. *The King,* she suddenly remembered, pulling back from Ryon, and opening her eyes. "What happened to the King? Where is he?"

Ryon brushed a strand of hair behind her ear and smiled that heart-stopping smile of his. "You mean the *new* King," he said. "You're looking at him."

Laina drew back, her brows knitted in confusion, but

Ryon only chuckled. "There's a lot I need to explain to you. But *later*. For now, I just want to hold you."

As he pulled her into his arms, wrapping them tightly around her, she couldn't help but smile. Six months ago, she thought the curve of a smile would never grace her lips again, yet here she was. She pulled back and glanced up at Ryon, at those golden-brown eyes she had come to love. He'd showed her that the world was so much bigger than she'd first thought. He'd saved her, protected her, supported her. Her smile widened when he leaned down and kissed her lips once more. It was then that she realised how ironic this moment truly was. The first time she met Ryon, she had been prepared to die. But now that she had died, she was ready to start living.

EPILOGUE

"This is it. This is the place," Ryon said as he raked his gaze over the abandoned cottage before him. The moon blanketed the area in an eery light that reflected off the broken windows and the caved-in front door. The grass surrounding the home was now overgrown to the point that the small step up to the front door could barely be seen, but Ryon knew it was there. He remembered it. Just like he remembered his mother being thrown out of the cottage to meet the sun. Ryon lifted his scarred hand, the memories of that night returning as he felt Laina's hand on his back.

He glanced over at her, into her golden eyes, and smiled. A week had passed since the day she died, since the day the King died, and Ryon's reluctant reign began. He wasn't ready to be King. Hell, he never expected to be the King, but with the help of those around him, he was coming to terms with it.

He'd made many changes—ceased the war with the humans, reinstated the Shadows and the rules that King Cazimir revoked. He'd sent out a Garabitha wide search party for Zane, which so far had proven unsuccessful. He'd told the

Shadows about the transition process and how vampires retained their human memories, provided their King and maker didn't wipe their mind in the process—which was how the Shadows had no memories of their past, but Laina did.

He'd even learned that Reds weren't entirely lost, they were redeemable with regular feedings and compulsion when needed to keep them in check. Fynn helped to keep track of the Reds progress, and it turned out, the King had given the Reds accommodation in an abandoned boarding school near the palace. With Ryon's permission, Fynn had started up something of a rehabilitation there for those Reds that were willing to comply and control their blood lust. For those who had no interest however, they were given no choice—and those cells in the basement of the palace were put to good use.

And then there was Laina. She'd been...*amazing*. She'd embraced her new form, her new home in the mansion, and her new life—as Queen of the Vampires in Garabitha. And as *his* Queen. She had decided to keep her freelancing job as a graphic designer, even though her work hours had changed a little. And she'd even reached out to Max, checking in on him despite how he'd treated her. Hell, she was even making strides controlling her blood lust, although sometimes that was easier said than done when Brynn was in the room. Brynn was still coming to terms with the change and insisted on visiting the mansion almost every night—much to Kove's frustration, that was.

"I love you," Ryon whispered.

"I love you, too," Laina said with a smile that took his breath away.

"Get a room!" Fynn called out as a mix of wolf whistles and boos echoed from behind them. Ryon and Laina turned to see the Shadows approaching from where they had faded into the area. *They're here.* Ryon had explained where he was going tonight, but he never expected them to turn up.

"We're here if you need us," Kove said, his face a mask of seriousness as his gaze drifted beyond Ryon to the cottage. The Shadows—Fynn, Xavier, Malik, Rune, Damien, and Darick...and yes, even Kove—had all arrived to be there for him. To support him in what he was about to do. And his chest swelled with pride as he looked around at the males that he called his friends.

"Do you want me to come with you?" Laina asked. Ryon shook his head, his attention going back to Laina.

"No, I need to do this on my own." Ryon reached down and gave Laina's hand a squeeze before moving towards the cottage. The small step creaked under his shoe, and when he stepped past the front door that was hanging off its hinges, he realised it was likely kicked in the day the King came to the place and remained there ever since. A large hole in the ceiling where a tree branch had fallen through now allowed the moonlight to stream in and illuminate the room. But other than that, it was just as he remembered it—only now a film of dust, dirt and leaves covered every surface. The lounge, the small dining table for two, even the kitchen was left exactly how it was before everything happened.

He walked past the lounge and towards the hallway that led to the bedrooms. The aged wood groaned underneath his weight with each step, and when he heard a 'thunk', he knew he'd found what he was looking for. He knelt down to see a small crevice between two planks and reached out, pulling it loose. His chest tightened when his gaze landed on a folded piece of paper that sat underneath. Swallowing down the knot in his throat, he hesitated a moment but then unfolded it, lifting it to the moonlight to read.

Ryszard, my son.
   If you are reading this, then King Cazimir has come for me—for us. I am writing this so that you know the truth about your past. I just hope I have done enough. I hope I have taught you enough about the good in this world to keep you from entertaining the bad.
   I want you to know that Cazimir wasn't always like this. We loved each other once. We were young and free. He was a prince, and I was the daughter of a civilian. Neither one of us wanted to get married or be a part of the politics and confinements of royalty. But then I fell pregnant, and a small rebel group of vampires killed his parents—your grandparents. Things changed after that. Cazimir got his revenge, but he also got a taste for killing and power. He changed. He began to speak of marriage, of ruling the vampires and finding a way to rule over humans as well. After you were born, he became obsessed with his legacy and having a son that would one day rule the world.
   That was when I left. I wanted peace for you, but Cazimir wanted you to have power. I fled Ladwick and came here before you were

old enough to remember your father, but today, they found us. They found me. I was at the markets while you were resting, and a civilian vampire recognised me. I tried to stay hidden, but word spread far and wide that the King was searching for us, so it was only a matter of time.

As I write this, I have no knowledge of when they'll come, but I have no doubt that they will. I have invited my oldest and most trusted friend to come here tonight, and I will plead with him to take care of you and keep you hidden. And I pray to the human God that he does. You have a kindness inside of you that Cazimir never did. You're better than him in every way.

With all my heart.
Your mother, Amaris

Ryon sucked in a breath as he finished reading the letter. And it was only after he'd read through it two more times that he folded it up. He placed the plank back where it had been but kept the letter in his palm. He stood and glanced around with a heavy heart as he remembered the way his mother was dragged down this very hallway where he stood.

He swallowed hard and followed the route she'd been dragged, down the hallway and into the living room before she was pushed out of the door and into the sun. Ryon made his way back out of the house and over to the overgrown grass area where he'd watched his mother become nothing more than ash. He knelt and placed a hand on the cool, damp ground before him. He searched for some sort of evidence or marking on the ground to signify his mother's resting place. But of course, there was nothing.

Ryon sensed Laina's presence before he felt her warm hand on his shoulder. He glanced up at her with a smile that he hoped was reassuring before she gave his shoulder a squeeze and stepped back. His gaze caught Kove behind her, and he watched in momentary confusion as Kove made his way over, squeezed Ryon's shoulder, and stepped back. One by one, each of his fellow enforcers, his Shadow members', and his friends, all stepped up and gave his shoulder a supportive squeeze. No words were necessary as their actions spoke volumes.

He took another moment to glance down at the ground before he stood and found Fynn in the darkness.

"Do you have a light?" he asked. To Ryon's surprise, Fynn reached into his pocket and handed over the lighter without any questions.

Making his way over to the house, Ryon exhaled and lifted his scarred hand. He'd hated seeing the damaged skin there, but now, the burns were a symbol of what he'd done for those he loved. A representation of his strength and loyalty. And he would wear them with pride.

Ryon took the lighter and held his mother's letter up to the ignited flame. He would remember her for being the strong and proud woman that she was, not the woman who feared for her life and her son's life, in the letter. Throwing the engulfed letter into the open doorway, Ryon moved back and watched as the small cottage slowly caught flame. There was a sadness in watching the remnants of his early life fall to ash, but it was time for a fresh start. Time for a new legacy.

Laina's arms came around his waist, and he pulled her in beside him, leaning down to kiss the top of her head. "Are you sure you want it to end this way?" she asked quietly as the smoke began to billow out of the home.

"It's not the end," he said, glancing at the flames. "This was *their* story." He turned back to her, and he couldn't hold back the smile when he said, "ours hasn't been written yet."

The End

NEXT IN THE SERIES

Ready for Kove's story?
Book 2 in the Protected by the Shadows series available now.

Loyal to the Past

Scan the QR code to start reading now!

ABOUT THE AUTHOR

N.A. Rose lives in Australia with her husband, children and some pet fish that her kids promised to take care of, but never have. When she isn't busy... *wait, let's rephrase that.* When she's not at her day job, chauffeuring the kids to and from school or activities, working on her next book or cleaning the damn fish tank, she can be found with her head in a book and a coffee in her hand (or maybe a glass of wine).

Learn more about N.A. Rose at www.naroseauthor.com or scan the below QR code to sign up to her newsletter for sneak peeks and exclusive content on upcoming books.

facebook.com/n.a.roseauthor

instagram.com/n.a.roseauthor

tiktok.com/@narosewriter

Made in the USA
Monee, IL
20 March 2025

14320307R10146